FIGHTING Chance

LACEY SAVAGE

ELLORA'S CAVE
ROMANTICA PUBLISHING

What the critics are saying...

ℬ

5 Hearts! "Lacey Savage never disappoints. This story will keep you on the edge of your seat, wondering what will happen next. And the sex scenes are totally hot and well written with sensuality and so much heat. […] I can't recommend this book enough." ~ *The Romance Studio Reviews*

5 Tattoos! "From start to finish *Fighting Chance* will have you on a thrilling, adventurous ride that will leave you breathless and screaming for more. […] Lacey Savage has crafted a fantastic start with her *Chance Encounters* series and I excitedly look forward to her next invigorating installment."
~ *Erotic Escapades Reviews*

4.5 Stars! "Lacey Savage has written quite an exciting and romantic story to begin the *Chance Encounters* series. […] I quite enjoyed the dark ambiance and the meticulous details of this story. The realism helped to connect this reader with all the characters in this tale. […] A definite keeper!" ~ *Just Erotic Romance Reviews*

4 Blue Ribbons! "*Fighting Chance* is not your average paranormal tale. […] Readers will enjoy this tale of paranormal love and passion that is sure to be a favorite." ~ *Romance Junkies Reviews*

An Ellora's Cave Romantica Publication

www.ellorascave.com

Fighting Chance

ISBN 9781419957543
ALL RIGHTS RESERVED.
Fighting Chance Copyright © 2007 Lacey Savage
Edited by Mary Moran.
Photography and cover art by Les Byerley.

This book printed in the U.S.A. by Jasmine-Jade Enterprises, LLC.

Electronic book Publication February 2007
Trade paperback Publication March 2008

Also by Lacey Savage

All the King's Men
Ghostly Awakening
Wed and Wanton

About the Author

෨

Award-winning author Lacey Savage loves to write about her dreams—or more specifically, she loves to breathe life into her steamy fantasies (and she's got plenty!). She pens erotic tales of true love and mythical destiny, peopled with strong alpha heroes and feisty heroines. A hopeless romantic, Lacey loves writing about the intimate, sensual side of relationships. She currently resides in Ottawa, Canada, with her loving husband and the mischievous cat.

Lacey welcomes comments from readers. You can find her website and email address on her author bio page at www.ellorascave.com.

Tell Us What You Think

We appreciate hearing reader opinions about our books. You can email us at Comments@EllorasCave.com.

FIGHTING CHANCE

જી

Trademarks Acknowledgement

ဆ

The author acknowledges the trademarked status and trademark owners of the following wordmarks mentioned in this work of fiction:

Brady Bunch, The: CBS Studios Inc.

Ford: Ford Motor Company

Google: Google Inc.

Harvard: Harvard College Corporation

Mission Impossible: Paramount Pictures Corporation

New York Daily: New York News Inc.

New York Post: NYP Holdings Inc.

Chapter One

ꙮ

Three hundred years ago, the sight of two naked women sprawled across a wide cherry-wood desk would have made Tristan Chance's cock hard enough to ache.

Tonight, he barely glanced at them. The cloying odors of sweat, arousal and too much perfume dripped off their bodies in nauseating waves, clogging his throat. Stronger still, another unmistakable scent wafted to Tristan's sensitive nose from the other side of the desk.

Fear.

"Tell me, Dick," Tristan said, leaning back in the oversized leather chair and crossing one ankle over his knee, "what made you think you could gamble with the big boys?"

Richard Gelling paled visibly under Tristan's scrutiny. He tugged at his black tie, his bandaged fingers fumbling with the tight knot. "It started with a thousand bucks. That's it. Just a measly grand."

"Then why do you need me?"

"Hey, y'know how it is." The man revealed a gap-toothed smile but his dark beady eyes glittered with the obvious hatred lurking beneath the easygoing demeanor. "Lose a thousand here, a thousand there. It never works out the way you planned." He pointed to the wall separating his office from the Bitter Sweet lounge. "Just tonight I lost my solo act. I've got no music out there because she walked off in the middle of a set. You think I planned that?"

"That's an easy problem to fix, Dick. I bet there are ten thousand people in New York who can carry a tune."

Richard blew out a breath. The stench of stale onion made Tristan grit his teeth.

"And how does that help me?" Richard asked. "I've got standards. My customers expect the best. Whoever I hire has to be able to sing, sure, but there's more to it than that. She has to be a college kid, rail thin, with a set of breasts fresh off the plastic surgeon's table and an ass I can bounce a quarter off."

Tristan flattened his lips into a thin, straight line and focused his attention beyond the man's head to the pair of hardwood paddles that decorated the back wall.

Richard cleared his throat. "Err…right. Look, won't you have something? My girls can give you anything you need."

Tristan raised an eyebrow and returned his gaze to the man's face. "I sincerely doubt that."

"What's your pleasure? There's sushi on Camille, if you like that sort of thing. Me, I never could get used to the taste." He leaned forward and dropped his voice to a confidential whisper. "If I wanted the taste of pussy, I'd eat pussy, y'know?" He chuckled then continued when Tristan didn't reply. "There's plenty of fruit on Brandi, and she's got chocolate melting in her bellybutton."

Richard grinned again, bobbing his head in eager invitation. Tristan spared the women a second glance. They both stared intently up at the ceiling, studiously avoiding eye contact. A peroxide-perfect blonde and a redhead barely old enough to step into a place with a legal liquor license lay motionless on the desk, legs entwined, facing in opposite directions. Food had been artfully arranged over their bodies, ranging from grapefruit slices on the redhead's breasts to cheese wedges in the shape of a smile on the blonde's stomach, and everything in between.

Two years ago, when Richard opened Bitter Sweet, no one had expected the tacky lounge to become the hottest nightspot in New York City. Yet word of the unusual cuisine and its shameless presentation had spread rapidly.

Although food critics had blasted the place as being vulgar and obscene, not to mention in violation of at least a few health codes, Bitter Sweet's popularity grew quickly. Within a couple of months, men began lining up hours before the lounge opened for the privilege of eating off some of the most gorgeous women in the city.

"You're not a poor man, Dick. I wouldn't be here if we were talking about a paltry amount."

Richard licked his thin lips and hung his head. His mop of brown hair flopped over his forehead, hiding his eyes. "It got out of hand, all right? Is that what you want to hear?"

"Lies and half truths aren't the foundation for an honest business arrangement. Maybe you're not familiar with that concept, but that's not my concern." Tristan steepled his hands in front of his chin and leaned forward. "How much do you owe?"

The stench of fear intensified and Tristan fought the urge to turn his head from it. "How much?" he repeated.

Richard mumbled a number under his breath, so softly that even the two women wouldn't have been able to make out the amount. Tristan's acute hearing picked up the words clearly but he wanted Richard to fully acknowledge the exorbitant sum.

"Don't make me ask you again."

"Fine!" Richard's head shot up, his small, dark eyes narrowing in distaste. "Twelve million dollars, okay? Twelve."

The blonde shifted and the wooden desk creaked beneath her weight. Richard shot her a menacing look. Her eyelids drifted closed and she stilled her movements, the slightly elevated rate of her breathing the only indication she was listening.

"That's better," Tristan said.

Relief flooded Richard's features. "So you'll do it? You'll help me?"

"Help you? No. But I will draw up some papers if we agree on a couple of conditions. This is a business deal, Dick, not a favor between friends. You will pay me back the agreed upon amount at regular intervals or else a couple of broken fingers will be the least of your worries."

"You have a flare for the dramatic, don't you?" Richard tugged at his tie again, the gesture revealing a fat vein that throbbed in his neck. This time Tristan did look away.

"There are a few things you should know before you agree." He held up his index finger. "One, for twelve million dollars, I want a ten percent stake in Bitter Sweet."

Richard gulped. "Ten percent? That's—"

"Not negotiable." He added a second finger to the first. "Two, you should be aware that all my contracts come with a hidden IOU clause."

A groan echoed through the room. "I heard about that. Some saint you are."

Tristan hid his grin. Hiring a public relations consultant had done wonders for his reputation. Now people not only feared him but also whispered his nickname reverently in closed circles, a name his rep had chosen and he'd come to like. Word traveled quickly and business had been booming for the past few years. He had to remember to give Marie a raise.

"You'll be able to take a look at the clause before you sign of course, but it's simple really. You or any of your descendants owe me or any of my descendants, one…let's call it a favor. The clause is binding for as long as our bloodlines last or until I come calling."

Richard shot him a sharp look. "What kind of favor? I won't have to kill anyone, will I?"

"I can't even begin to speculate what I might need from you. But rest assured, if you're thinking about hiding out somewhere I won't be able to find you, that's impossible.

There is no place on this earth that's beyond my reach. You understand?"

"And if I refuse to do as you command, my lord?" Sarcasm dripped from Richard's voice but his body remained tense, muscles rigid.

Tristan grinned, flashing his fangs for only a second.

A second was long enough. The man's jaw dropped open. Terror, swift and paralyzing, swept across his features, freezing his face in a motionless grimace.

"You die."

* * * * *

An hour later, Tristan slipped a signed agreement into the inside pocket of his suit jacket and left Richard's office breathing a sigh of relief. The informal paperwork didn't cover the full amount of twelve million dollars—he'd need his lawyers for that—but it served as a reminder that neither Richard nor Tristan could back out of the deal. For his show of good faith, Tristan had signed a check for five hundred thousand, which guaranteed that Richard kept most of his body parts intact until the rest of the contract could be drawn up.

Ignoring the guards posted outside Richard's door, Tristan strode down the length of the narrow hall leading to the lounge where loud, boisterous voices swept over him from every side. Saturdays were the busiest night of the week at Bitter Sweet. The last article he'd read in the *New York Daily* warned men to be prepared to wait as long as six hours for a table on a Saturday. Sweeping his gaze over the crowded lounge, Tristan couldn't understand why.

The dim, private atmosphere of the place was inviting enough, in a tacky, oversexed kind of way. Blue neon lights glittered from golden sconces set in mosaic patterns against black-painted walls. Only the ceiling boasted bright color. A fresco portraying a luminous blue sky and nude women frolicking among the clouds stood out in stark contrast to the dark walls, the mahogany tables, the black leather seats.

Twenty-four tables, each seating six, had been arranged around the room. Unlike in Richard's office, only one woman lay on each table, her body strategically covered with artfully arranged food. None moved as men grabbed for the most tempting morsels—those covering their breasts and pelvic areas.

Against one wall, a mirrored bar held hundreds of bottles and upturned crystal glasses. In the center of the room was a raised stage and a dance floor, but both stood empty. Tristan doubted the dance floor received much use. Unless they worked here, women didn't come to Bitter Sweet and Tristan supposed the lounge's clientele had a reputation to uphold and wouldn't be caught dead dancing with one another, no matter how many of those bottles lining the bar they'd indulged in.

Although the odors tickling his nose were milder here than they'd been in Richard's small office, he still easily distinguished the unmistakable scents of arousal, body heat, tobacco and too much alcohol.

He walked through the crowd, trying to avoid brushing against anyone as he passed. As much as the smells revolted him though, the sounds human bodies made intrigued and enticed him. In particular, the soft vibration of blood rushing through thick veins made his mouth water.

Gritting his teeth, Tristan glanced at his watch. The first light of dawn would make an appearance in a couple of hours. He'd indulged in a fleeting taste of nourishing blood before the meeting but he'd need a full meal before sunrise.

A waiter dressed in black slacks and a turtleneck bore a metal tray on which a dozen martini glasses balanced precariously. Swirling liquid gleamed a navy blue in each of them. The man stopped beside Tristan and tilted his head in invitation. "On the house."

"No need. I'm leaving."

The waiter chuckled. "No one leaves this place before closing time. You'd have to be a fool to leave before all the food is gone."

"I don't like what's on the menu."

"Hey, suit yourself, man. There are plenty of gay bars down the street."

Tristan didn't bother explaining. It didn't matter what the waiter thought and besides, feeding was feeding. Women were much easier to feed upon but a gay man would easily do in a pinch.

Elbowing his way past a middle-aged man wearing a Hawaiian shirt, Tristan had almost reached the door when he spotted the woman lying on a table situated in the darkest corner of the room.

His mouth went dry. He stopped in mid-stride, instantly alert.

It wasn't just that she was stunning, though she certainly was that. A riot of midnight-black curls fell in tight waves around her creamy shoulders, drawing his attention to the faint blue vein pulsing at the side of her slender throat.

No, what really made the breath catch in his throat was the knowledge that he'd seen her twice before, just that evening. As he'd climbed into his limo, he'd noticed her crossing the street against the light. A couple of hours later he'd bumped into her again as he pushed past the waiting crowd to enter Bitter Sweet.

That's how it starts. The curse knows, Tristan. It gets you when you least expect it, with nothing more menacing than random sightings and coincidental run-ins.

Annoyed at himself for letting his younger brother's insistent ramblings intrude upon his thoughts, Tristan neared the table.

When he'd seen her outside, he'd been attracted to the way her long legs peeked out from under a knee-length jacket, flashing the barest hint of a metallic miniskirt. Now the only items camouflaging the perfection of her supple, lean body were the assembled bits of food and an abundance of gold jewelry. Rings, a long triple-strand necklace, bracelets, anklets and two toe rings shone against her pale skin.

As he drew closer, the air around her shifted. The men feasting upon her didn't notice but Tristan did. Energy sheltered her—an undulating tide of pure bright light that flowed and pulsed with the rhythmic rise and fall of her chest. He blinked hard, trying to dispel the vision, but it didn't fade. Instead, the light intensified as he stopped inches away from her.

That's when he noticed she had her eyes closed. The other women had all focused intently upon the ceiling, but her lashes didn't as much as flutter. On impulse, Tristan reached out and stroked the tender skin at the hollow dip of her collarbone.

"No touching," she said. Her throaty, confident voice sent a jolt of heat to his groin. She sounded like a woman used to being admired, a woman utterly unashamed in her nudity and comfortable in her own skin. These days, that was practically a miracle. "You may grab the food," she continued, "and if your hand brushes against me once, fine. But fondling is entirely out of the question."

"Is that the establishment's rule or yours?"

She lifted a slender shoulder in a delicate half shrug, but she didn't smile. At last she opened her eyelids a fraction. When she spotted him, panic flashed in her hazel eyes.

"Oh God," she whispered in a voice so low he was certain only he could hear. "It's really you, isn't it?"

A sigh hitched in Tristan's throat. How did she know him? He was sure he didn't know her.

"Leave us," he said to the men gathered around the table. Until that moment, they'd hardly given him a second glance, content to elbow each other and snicker in delight as they uncovered inch after flawless inch of the woman's satiny skin.

"Hey, man, this is our table. Do you have any idea how much we paid to get in here tonight?"

"That's really none of my concern." Tristan eyed the man closest to him, a kid barely out of college. A chain extended from his nose to his ear, hooked through two identical rings. Briefly Tristan pictured himself yanking that chain, tossing the man toward the door and taking his spot.

"Well, it sure as hell is mine," a man built like a pro football player said from across the table. He pushed his chair back and rose to his full height, a head taller than Tristan's six feet. His upper lip curling in a snarl, the man crossed his brawny arms across his chest. The scowl etched on his features made Tristan think of a pit bull in heat.

"Gentlemen, we can do this the easy way or we can do it the hard way. The choice is yours."

Pit Bull laughed and the harsh sound carried above the loud, gregarious chatter permeating the lounge. "I never do anything the easy way."

Tristan sighed and glanced down at the woman. She hadn't moved but her eyes remained open and she watched the events unfolding around her with obvious interest.

"Don't ask me," she said. "I get paid no matter which one of you sits here."

"It's not a party unless there are at least six men involved, right, sweetheart?" The college kid guffawed at his innuendo.

That gave Tristan all the excuse he needed to start with him. Giving in to his earlier impulse to literally yank the kid's chain would have made too much of a mess so he settled for clutching the back of his neck in an iron grip and lifting him to his feet.

"What the fuck, man?" The confident swagger had drained out of his voice, leaving behind a frightened high pitch.

"Your friend didn't like the choices I offered. Maybe the rest of you would like to rethink your options."

Still dangling the guy two inches off the ground, Tristan swung around to face Pit Bull, who had already begun to move. "So much for that idea."

He stood perfectly still until Pit Bull came close enough to strike then threw the college kid at him with enough force to knock them both backward. They tumbled together in a sprawl of arms and legs, knocking a waiter off his feet in the process. The clatter of glass and metal ringing against the floor brought with it a deep, enveloping silence that draped over the room.

People stood and gaped, meals and chatter forgotten. A few even kneeled beside the men on the ground and tried to help. Only the women hadn't moved from their spots on the tables. They'd obviously been well trained and perhaps were no strangers to the occasional scuffle.

"Now will you leave?" Tristan asked. "Or would you like another demonstration?"

"No, dude, we're cool." A third man, this one dressed in a flamboyant pink shirt, held both hands up in the air in the international gesture of surrender. "We were just leaving anyway."

Tristan gave a short nod then turned to the rest of the crowd, somewhat relieved to notice they'd already returned to their meals. He hadn't intended to fight a hundred people. He'd only wanted a minute alone with this woman.

A woman who obviously knew him.

Just as his blood knew her. Recognition had swept over his senses each time he'd seen her but until now he'd been too distracted to notice. At first he'd thought she simply reminded him of someone but he couldn't think of anyone with her striking full lips, small upturned nose, high cheekbones and piercing hazel eyes.

Logically, none of this made any sense. Tristan was certain he'd never laid eyes on her before tonight. What was it Hayden had said? The curse starts with odd coincidences and chance encounters?

That was stupid. A curse hadn't made them meet tonight. Simple proximity did. He'd seen her on the street then in front of the lounge and finally *in* the lounge. New York wasn't really that big a city. It wasn't completely improbable that two people would run into each other.

Sitting in the newly vacated leather chair, Tristan waited until the woman's gaze turned to him again. She'd been trying to avoid him but whether because of the violent display she'd just witnessed or something else, he wasn't sure.

"How do you know me?" Tristan asked at last.

She looked away and swept the tip of her pink tongue over her lower lip. The innocent gesture made heat coil low in Tristan's stomach. He pictured that tongue sweeping over his cock, dipping into the slit and slowly licking the bead of moisture gathered there.

"I...I don't."

"That's not the impression you gave earlier."

Embedding her teeth into her lower lip, she didn't answer. Her gaze returned to the ceiling.

Tristan leaned forward, noting as he did so that no trace of the chemical perfume so many women preferred these days masked her natural scent. Her delicate feminine aroma didn't offend his sensitive nose. Instead, it made him lean in to better capture the fragrance. Delicate musky odor mingled with something sweet and elusive to form an ambrosial perfume to which his body responded on a primal level.

"No one says 'it's really you, isn't it' without meaning it. Who do you think I am?"

A flush crept up her neck to settle into the apples of her cheeks. "You're not going to give up, are you?"

"I don't see why I should."

She glared at him then, her eyes flashing with barely contained annoyance. "Do you always get your own way?"

He didn't try to hide the proud smile that tugged at his lips. "Always."

"Fine then, if you really want to know, I thought you were someone else. For a moment, I thought I recognized you."

It felt as though I'd waited for you my whole life.

The thought flashed through Tristan's mind as vivid as though it had been his own. But it hadn't. He'd heard her voice—throaty and sensual—as the phrase formed in his mind.

Stunned, he leaned back in his chair. He'd never been able to read minds before. He'd heard vampires grew in power as they aged, that sometimes they developed talents they hadn't previously possessed, but he'd had no idea telepathy was possible with humans.

He'd always been able to communicate telepathically with his two brothers but that was more like thought transference. He could send them his thoughts but he couldn't read theirs unless they projected them to him. Besides, his brothers were part of his bloodline, linked together for eternity. Until a few hours ago, he hadn't even known this woman existed.

She grimaced, as though fighting an internal battle and losing.

That was a really dumb thing to think, Lara. Get a grip!

"Lara," he repeated, trying her name out on his tongue. He liked the feel of it rolling from his mouth.

"How do you know my name?" She pursed her lips as she turned her head, the movement dislodging a cherry from the valley between her full breasts. It rolled off the table and fell to the ground.

Tristan shrugged. "It's not much of a secret."

Tristan rubbed the bridge of his nose. "I think I worked with a Montgomery once, a century ago. At the time, he needed a pretty hefty sum to leave London in a hurry after he slept with the wife of a parliamentary representative of some sort, if I remember correctly."

"It wasn't sleeping with the woman that did him in. It was getting caught."

Tristan shook his head in silent admonishment but he smiled anyway. "So what do they want with me? My IOU is still outstanding."

"That's exactly why this is so bizarre." Marie paused long enough to take a gulp of coffee. "They're willing to add another promise to their previous arrangement."

"A second IOU?" Tristan frowned. "They must be desperate."

"That's what I gathered. It seems Montgomery did well for himself in the new world. He started a small bed and breakfast in 1911, which he upgraded to an inn a few years later. Pretty soon he had a hotel and then another and another. Now his descendants are carrying on the family tradition."

"Wait a second. Gregory Montgomery, sheepherder, started Montgomery Suites?"

"Looks that way, boss."

Admiration didn't often catch Tristan by surprise but he had to admit Gregory had exceeded his expectations. Although he now kept careful tabs on all his clients, he'd written off the Montgomerys long ago. When Gregory had first approached him, Tristan had only been running his new enterprise for eight months. Using the few thousand dollars he'd managed to save, he'd begun helping people like Montgomery who couldn't help themselves.

And helping *himself* in the process.

His meager earnings grew at a considerable rate. Soon Tristan had made a name for himself, but it wasn't until he hired Marie that the business really took off.

"Monday, midnight. Got it. Anything else?"

"That's it. I'll leave the address on your desk."

He clicked the cell phone off and turned to Lara, anticipation zinging through his bloodstream.

The table was empty.

He moved quickly but found only a few chocolate smears, some grapefruit and a couple of blackberries dripping with honey in her wake. Fists clenched at his sides, he dashed between tables and stormed into Richard's office.

He found the man kneeling on his desk between a pair of long legs, mouth clamped tightly against the redhead's pussy. The blonde stood off to one side, one hand pinching a nipple, the other burrowed between her thighs. The room reeked of sex.

"Funny, I didn't see that on the menu," Tristan said, slamming the door behind him.

Richard's head jerked up and alarm swept over his face. Tristan lifted a hand to silence him before he spoke. "I'm not here to cash in. Not yet, anyway," he added casually. "I need some information on one of your employees."

Relief made Richard's body sag. He slapped his companion's thigh and the woman sat up. The blonde looped her arm through the redhead's and they beamed identical come-hither smiles at Tristan before leaving through the side door.

Richard wiped the back of his hand over his mouth and slumped in his chair. "What do you want to know?"

"One of your…what do you call them? Models?"

Richard wiggled his eyebrows suggestively. "Servers."

"I'm looking for the one who works the corner table by the door. About five feet eight, curly black hair, hazel eyes, pale skin, lots of jewelry."

Richard's thin lips pulled back to reveal a predatory smile. "You've got good taste but you aim too high, my friend.

In the year she's worked here, I haven't seen anyone get that close to her."

"Let me worry about that. Who is she?"

"That's Lara Montgomery."

Tristan forced a laugh but a sinking feeling had already begun to form in the pit of his stomach. "Let me guess. Her father owns the Montgomery Suites chain of hotels."

"That's the one. I guess that makes her an heiress, like that Hilton girl... What's her name? Milan? Venice?"

"Paris."

"Yeah, right." Richard leaned forward in his chair. "What I wouldn't give to have her serving at Bitter Sweet. How much do you think people would pay for a two-for-one heiress special?"

His chuckle followed Tristan to the door.

"Don't make too many plans you may not be able to keep," Tristan called out from the hallway. "I *will* come after you."

Chapter Two

ඬ

Lara pushed her way through the revolving door and stepped into the dazzling lobby of the Montgomery Suites corporate headquarters situated on Manhattan's Upper East Side. As always, the brilliant white marble made her think of her father's cold eyes and a chill ran up her spine.

Concentrating on placing one foot in front of the other, Lara beamed a smile at the security guard sitting behind the wide desk in front of the elevators. "Good evening, Michael. My father's expecting me."

The guard positioned the logbook in front of her and indicated where to sign. "Odd time for a meeting."

Lara frowned. She'd been thinking the same thing ever since her father's phone call a few hours earlier. Although she'd spent the morning here at the office, he hadn't mentioned a possible business meeting after hours. Yet their earlier conversation had led her to believe this was not a last-minute arrangement.

Nothing about this should have surprised her. As usual, her father didn't share any information with his offspring until the last possible moment.

"Yeah, well, you know the Montgomerys," she said, trying to keep her tone light. "We don't do anything the easy way."

The words were barely out of her mouth when a startling image of the man she'd met at Bitter Sweet flashed through her mind. She remembered the way he'd looked—long, unbound hair falling over her shoulders, the straight, determined line of his full lips emphasized by shadows—and felt her nipples tighten.

His words rang clearly through her mind. *We can do this the easy way or we can do it the hard way. The choice is yours.*

Considering she hadn't been able to go more than ten minutes at a time without thinking about him since that night, she knew she'd made her choice. The realization was both infuriating and terrifying. In the year she'd worked at Bitter Sweet, she'd never been even remotely tempted to get close to a client. But there was something about that man…something startlingly familiar and infinitely arousing that had made a definite impression.

Michael's good-natured chuckle brought her back to the present. He inclined his head toward the elevators. "They're waiting for you in the main boardroom."

Lara spun on her heel, her finger on the elevator button. "They?" she repeated. "Who else is here?"

"So far only your brother but I'm told they're expecting someone else. I was given a name but it doesn't mean anything to me."

The bell chimed as the doors slid open. "What's the name?"

"Tristan Chance."

The name meant nothing to her either. "Thanks, Michael. Have a good shift."

She pressed the button to the twelfth floor then turned to inspect her appearance in the full-length mirror that covered all four walls of the spacious elevator. The pinstriped suit she'd chosen suited her new position. It hugged her curves but the skirt brushed the tops of her knees in a modest length of which her father would approve.

A curly strand had escaped the neat bun she'd used to tame her wild mane but there wasn't much she could do about it now. Tucking it behind her ear, she frowned then tugged on the hem of her suit jacket. The white silk shirt she wore peeked from the V of her lapel. She'd opted to leave two buttons undone but quickly reconsidered and buttoned one before the elevator doors opened.

Sweat coated her palms and she wiped them quickly on her skirt. As she neared the boardroom, her pulse began to race, faster and faster as a direct result of her proximity to her father. Why the man still affected her this way after all these years, she didn't know. An MBA in accounting should have been proof enough that she was capable of handling this job and more.

Yet her need to prove herself to her father was just as strong now as it had been when she was a wide-eyed child, eager to please. Within her, that same need now battled with the fierce desire to defy him.

She worked at Bitter Sweet because it was the one thing she could do that wasn't connected to the Montgomery family name. Besides, she was sure her father and brother would never stoop so low as to step foot in the establishment. She doubted any of her father's acquaintances would recognized the straitlaced daughter of the hotel tycoon in the nude model serving their food, but if by some miracle someone did, she figured denying having ever heard of the place would be easy enough.

Her father would believe her. The alternative would be too horrible for him to contemplate.

Taking one last deep breath to steel her nerves, she pushed open the set of double doors and stepped into the boardroom. The hushed conversation stopped when she walked in and two sets of identical steely gray eyes turned to focus on her.

Her father looked the part of the powerful business entrepreneur, Lara thought as she closed the door behind her. Now in his sixties, the aura of power surrounding him had only intensified as he'd aged. His white hair and the fine lines around his mouth and eyes gave him the no-nonsense appearance of someone used to getting his way.

"Hi, Dad. Elias." She nodded to each of them.

Her brother's dark good looks were boyish in comparison to their father's. His round cheeks and ruddy complexion made people underestimate him upon their first meeting. It didn't take them long to realize they'd underrated Elias Montgomery however. In the ten years he'd been vice-CEO of Montgomery Suites, he'd rapidly gained a reputation as a ruthless businessman with few qualms and fewer morals.

"Lara," her father acknowledged at last. "Don't I pay you enough to buy a decent suit?"

Lara stiffened. She bit her tongue to prevent a clever retort that would only anger him further. "I thought this would be appropriate for a midnight meeting."

"Maybe if you were hoping to end the meeting on your back," Elias said. The pointed look he shared with their father made Lara grit her teeth to bite off the scathing retort burning her tongue.

She fisted her hands at her sides, determined to ignore the comment. She'd spent years trying to come to terms with the fact that no matter how many degrees she earned, she'd never be good enough for either of them. Not for the first time, she wondered if perhaps she should just walk out and never return. Her job at Bitter Sweet paid well enough to get by. Sure, losing half of her inheritance would take some getting used to but she knew she could adjust.

Who are you kidding? You'd never walk away.

She grimaced, knowing that was true. She'd worked too hard to convince her father she was as capable as Elias of running the business when the time came to give up because of a nasty comment or two.

Of course there may not be anything left of Montgomery Suites by then, making this entire exercise a complete waste of her time.

Swallowing hard, Lara walked past the array of windows that offered a perfect view of the New York City skyline to take her customary seat at her father's left. As Stephen Montgomery's right-hand man, Elias always held the matching seat.

"So who's Tristan Chance?" she asked as she placed her briefcase on the floor beside her chair.

Elias opened his mouth but another voice—a deeper, infinitely sexier voice—answered. "I think that's my cue."

Lara froze, still leaning over her briefcase. She closed her eyes and swallowed back a groan.

It can't be. It just can't be.

"Why can't it?"

Startled, Lara practically jumped out of her seat. She hadn't said that out loud, had she?

"Mr. Chance, how good of you to join us." Her father rose and extended his hand. Tristan shook it then turned to Elias and did the same. Knowing she couldn't postpone it any longer, Lara rose to her feet, grateful for the thick wooden table that hid her buckling knees.

She looked up into a startlingly familiar pair of eyes. Green flecked with gold, his imposing stare made her feel as though he could see right through her. Though she hadn't believed it possible, he looked even better now than he had two nights ago. He still wore a suit, but this one was black instead of charcoal. It matched his long black hair. The night they met, he'd worn his hair loose and it had framed his face as he'd bent over her. Tonight, he'd pulled it back in a low ponytail.

His lips curved upward in a slow, sensual smile that made her tongue sweep over her own lips in response. What would that mouth feel like beneath her own? His body on top of hers? His hands skimming down her spine to cup her ass and press her against his erection?

"I'm Tristan Chance." His outstretched hand drew hers like a magnet.

"Lara Montgomery," she said, relieved her voice didn't quiver.

He curled his large fingers around her hand and the impact of his touch nearly sent her reeling.

His skin was cold but his firm grip held her anchored in place. She clenched her teeth as a tremor ran through her, zinging along her veins and burrowing between her legs. Her clit became a sensitive, throbbing nub. Her breasts felt heavy, aching to be touched.

A distant corner of her brain registered that Tristan's thumb formed small, sensual circles against the back of her hand. Her nipples beaded into hard points. Prickles of awareness danced along her nerve endings and she became vaguely cognizant of the slick, sticky puddle forming between her legs.

Oh God. This can't be happening.

Abruptly, he released her. She fell backward, thankful for the chair that cushioned her landing.

"Do you two know each other?" Disapproval radiated from her father in waves, enveloping her in the ardent displeasure with which she'd become so familiar over the years.

"No."

"Yes."

They'd spoken at once and Lara sent a menacing glare Tristan's way. She bit her lower lip in an abysmal effort to keep him from seeing how much his presence unnerved her.

Too late for that, Lara.

Tristan's gaze flickered over her body. "My mistake. For a moment, I thought I recognized you."

She recalled saying those same words to him when they'd met, except in her case, they'd been true. The moment she'd laid eyes on him, a terrifying and alien feeling of recognition had slammed into her. For a brief moment, she'd been convinced she not only knew him but that she'd been *waiting* for him. Expecting him.

Absurd. The whole thing was completely absurd.

She gave a curt nod of acknowledgement. "Imagine that."

Before Tristan could say anything else, Elias gestured to the chair closest to him. "Please, have a seat and we'll get right down to it. We don't want to take up too much of your time."

Was it just her imagination or did she detect a tremor in her brother's voice? Lara frowned. She couldn't remember ever hearing Elias sound nervous in front of anyone.

Tristan ignored him. He held Lara's gaze until the silence became uncomfortable then walked around the long table and pulled out the chair closest to her.

She nearly groaned. If she'd hoped to make her father believe she and Tristan were complete strangers, his behavior certainly wasn't helping.

"I think we all know why I'm here," Tristan said when he was seated. He pulled his chair close to the table and nudged it closer to her. Their calves brushed against each other and she yanked her leg back, slamming her knee into the tabletop in the process.

"Fuck," she murmured under her breath.

Her father sent her a look that could melt steel. "You'll have to excuse my daughter, Mr. Chance. Her manners leave a lot to be desired."

Lara fought the urge to stick out her tongue. Instead, she smoothed a hand over her skirt and folded her hands in her lap. Her entire body hummed at the proximity of the man beside her. Just keeping her gaze locked on the pools of neon light spilling over the tabletop's dark sheen took every ounce of willpower she possessed.

"I'll get right to the point." Stephen Montgomery's voice boomed through the conference room. "Montgomery Suites is in trouble."

Ah. That explained the meeting, if not the odd hour. Lara had spent the last few months agonizing over the best way to cut costs without resulting to layoffs or closing down hotels. Her degree had at least made her father put her in charge of corporate finances, if reluctantly.

Still, the man had shut down every idea she'd had regarding the financial state of the company. The truth was, profits had been dropping steadily over the past ten years. This year they'd reached an all-time low while debts continued to rise. The company couldn't continue down this path for much longer.

But what did Tristan Chance have to offer that would change the inevitable course of the business?

"Our competitors have continued to get the upper hand," Stephen continued. "Their lowered prices combined with their customer loyalty rewards have made it impossible for us to compete in this aggressive industry. Until now."

He paused and took a deep breath. Lara drummed her fingernails on the tabletop, waiting for the inevitable bombshell. She'd seen him use this same strategy too many times to count. He'd heighten the tension in the room then drop a thunderbolt on his captive audience.

"We need your help, Mr. Chance. With your generous contribution, we can begin a nationwide advertising campaign and tie that in with a number of additional promotional endeavors. We can begin a massive renovation effort. We've even lined up partnerships between Montgomery Suites and other businesses—from Champagne producers to Egyptian-linen manufacturers. In a year, Montgomery Suites will be the elegant high-class chain of hotels it was meant to be."

"You'd need a lot of money for that," Lara blurted out before she could think better of it.

For once, her father didn't glare at her or tell her to shut up in so many words. His gaze remained fixed intently on Tristan. "And that's where Mr. Chance comes in."

Lara wasn't aware Tristan had moved his hand until he placed it on her knee. Not bothering with pantyhose now seemed like a really bad idea. She bit her lip to keep from moaning.

"How much?" Tristan asked.

Elias answered but his words didn't make sense. The sum was so absurd, Lara was certain she must have misunderstood.

She squinted, staring first at her brother then at her father, as though daring either one of them to repeat the insane amount.

"Seven hundred and fifty million dollars," Tristan said. "Is that all?"

Until a couple of years ago, Tristan had rarely dealt with amounts larger than a million dollars. People just didn't think in terms of taking out a long-term, multimillion dollar loan. No one wanted to owe that kind of money to a virtual stranger.

But Marie was damn good at her job. It had only taken her a few weeks to plant the necessary seeds of gossip around New York's high society. She'd made it clear Tristan could be counted on to help cover financial situations ranging from a private heart transplant to a kidnapping ransom and everything in between.

The sum of seven hundred and fifty million dollars however, was new even to him.

At his side, Lara's mouth gaped open as she stared at Montgomery Senior in horror. "You can't be serious."

"Like a heart attack," Elias answered. His easy grin didn't quite mask the calculating look in his dark eyes.

She shifted in her chair and met Tristan's gaze for the first time since they shook hands. "Tell them this is insane. You don't have that kind of money to lend." She paused and swallowed hard, the movement in her throat drawing his attention to her soft skin. "Do you?"

"I do."

She threw her hands in the air. "That's fantastic. All the work I've done over the past year, everything I've tried to do to get the company out of debt was irrelevant, wasn't it? You could have just called Mr. Fix-It in here at any time." She crossed her arms over her breasts. Even through the thick material of her jacket, he could see the faint outline of her hard nipples pressing against the tight constraints.

"I prefer The Saint," Tristan said, not bothering to hide a smile.

"The Saint," she repeated, shaking her head. "This is unbelievable."

"Once again, I must ask you to forgive my daughter's outburst," Stephen said, leaning forward in his chair. The frown lines around his thin lips spoke of a man who could probably count on one hand the number of genuine smiles he'd offered in the past year.

"Oh that's right. Please forgive me for being the voice of reason in this absurd meeting." Lara rose from her chair and walked to the full-length window behind them. The urge to turn his head and follow her movements nagged at Tristan but he kept his eyes fixed on Stephen's.

"I've brought some preliminary paperwork with me." Tristan reached into his suit jacket and pulled out a thick envelope. "This doesn't cover all the terms of the agreement but it is legally binding."

Elias made a grab for the envelope but Tristan held it just out of reach. "Before we sign anything, I need to go over a few key points."

"The silent IOU," Stephen supplied. His features suddenly looked drawn, as if the stress of seeing his business crumble had finally caught up to him.

"Precisely."

"The what?" Lara slid into the chair she'd vacated. She looked slightly more composed but her tightly bound hair had begun to escape the neat bun at the nape of her neck, reminding him a little more of the woman he'd met a few days ago.

He'd expected to see her here tonight but *this* woman looked nothing like the vixen who'd sprawled across the Bitter Sweet table, looking good enough to eat.

Pulsing excitement rippled through Tristan at the thought of her full breasts, her flat stomach, the full pink lips of her pussy he'd been able to discern beneath a strategically placed lettuce leaf and a towering mound of pineapple slices.

Shifting in his chair to hide his growing erection, Tristan had to work at stopping his smile from turning into a full-fledged grin. "I'm surprised you don't know about that, considering your family already owes me one."

"My family owes you nothing." She held her chin up as she spoke but her haughty glare wavered and the uncertainly in her tone hit him like a punch to the gut.

It didn't take a genius to figure out she didn't have the best relationship with her brother and father. She might have been a heiress but it was clear even to him that the real heir to the Montgomery empire was Elias, not Lara.

"That's enough." Stephen didn't shout but his voice commanded authority. "One more outburst like that and you'll no longer be privy to this meeting. Understood?"

Lara lowered her gaze to her lap. A vein twitched in her clenched jaw. He heard the blood rushing through her veins, her heart beating a wild rhythm in her chest.

Everything about her called to him on a savage, primal level. He wanted nothing more than to see her lying naked on the conference room table. This time though, there would be no food hiding her perfect body from view. And she *would* be the main course.

"Actually, no one's going anywhere." Tristan placed the sealed envelope in front of him. "I need all three signatures on this contract before I can go forward with the deal."

Shock flashed across Stephen's face for only a moment before he smoothed his features into his customary professional mask. "Why? I was told only I would need to sign. I wanted my children here so I could show them the kind of sacrifices I've made for this company my entire life. For their future." He growled low under his breath.

Not for my *future.*

Lara's thoughts had continued to come to Tristan in sporadic bursts when he least expected them. The sensation would have been unnerving if Tristan wasn't already used to sharing a telepathic link with his two younger brothers.

Tristan, Hayden and Alexander had been turned into vampires the same night. Like everything else the Chances did, they embraced immortality together, determined to conquer everything life threw at them — including death.

The three brothers had grown up together, first as children then later as fledgling vampires. Their thoughts were inexorably linked but the ability was based on physical proximity. As neither one of Tristan's brothers currently lived in New York, he couldn't hear their thoughts now.

A deep, familiar ache ran through him. He missed them both but he could hardly expect them to welcome his watchful, overprotective guardianship at the age of three hundred.

Lara licked her lips, giving Tristan a glimpse of her pink tongue and focusing his attention on her. The thought of that mouth, those lips, wrapped around his cock as she slowly and erotically licked up and down the length of his shaft made his rod stiffen farther. Just how much longer would this meeting last before he'd have a chance to have her all to himself?

"This is highly unusual," Tristan said, forcing his attention back to the deal at hand. "One contract per family line is my limit. Any more and it gets complicated, not to mention it becomes increasingly difficult to balance the risk with the reward."

He paused for a moment, allowing his gaze to sweep the room and settle on Lara. He wanted to leave no doubt in her mind that she was the main reason he was even considering this arrangement. "For you, I'm willing to make an exception."

He could have been speaking to any one of them or referring to the family as a whole. The pursed lips and drawn faces of the men as well as Lara's wide, bright eyes, told him they all knew he wasn't.

"For a price." Elias' easy smile was gone, replaced by a frown that mirrored his father's.

Tristan chuckled. "You didn't expect me to hand over seven hundred and fifty million dollars, wish you a nice day and then be on my way. Did you?"

Stephen let out a haggard sigh. "Let's hear your terms."

Tristan nodded and held up his index finger. "One. I want a seat on the board of directors and ten percent of all Montgomery Suites shares." He saw Stephen pale but he didn't stop long enough to give the man a chance to protest. A second finger joined the first. "And two, I want you all to sign silent IOUs."

"All of us?" Elias' startled whine would have been funny, if the terror on his features wasn't so sad. His fear had a thick, pungent odor to it.

Lara slammed both hands on the table, startling her brother. He shrank back farther in his chair. "Would someone please tell me what this silent IOU is?"

"It's a way for him to control us," Elias said, barely managing to hold back the tremor in his voice. "For as long as we live, we could be called on to perform a task for him. Any task of his choosing, no matter how dangerous or costly."

Lara gnawed her lower lip while she considered her brother's words. When she spoke, Tristan watched blood fill the white mark her teeth had left behind. "This hardly seems like a fair deal."

"You're right," Tristan said.

"I am?"

"She is?" Elias echoed.

"Absolutely. One lifespan may not be enough to collect from all of you, so the agreement is binding to your bloodline and to mine. Any of my descendants can also call upon any of yours if I haven't already done so."

Lara groaned. She let her head fall back against the headrest of the imposing leather seat. Her eyelids fluttered closed. Her blood ran hot and fast, the *swish* of it pounding in Tristan's own ears. Beneath the rhythmic pulse echoed something else, a beat of arousal that took him by surprise.

The knowledge that she wanted him even though he probably frightened her as much as he scared her brother made Tristan's muscles clench. For a brief moment, the tension in the room dissipated as he admired her lush curves through her tight, form-fitting suit. He had to admit, he preferred her Bitter Sweet uniform to the professional businesswoman look, though it would be a hell of a lot of fun to get her out of this one.

She opened her eyes and the searing glare she threw his way awakened every neglected nerve in his body.

"I won't do it," she said. She didn't tear her gaze from his, but she twisted her fingers together in her lap, the nervous gesture speaking volumes about her inner turmoil. "I won't sign."

"Lara…" Stephen's voice held warning and a hint of menace. "You're not going to ruin this for us, you understand? If you're worried about the IOU nonsense, don't be."

Tristan hid his smile. No doubt the senior Montgomery thought he could outsmart him. Perhaps he even thought he and his children could hide somewhere they'd never be found.

He'd seen it too many times before. Humans considered themselves so smart, so cunning. They had no idea they left trails everywhere they went. Technology made it incredibly easy to find someone and nature did the rest. Tristan could recognize a person's natural scent from miles away and then all he had to do was follow his noise right to their doorstep.

A rush of air escaped Lara's lips. "This can't be legal."

"I have a team of a dozen lawyers who draw up my contracts. I assure you, no one could find legal fault with it."

"That's why he calls the IOU a silent term." Elias sneered. "It's not in the contract."

"Well, that's not entirely true. It is in the contract and you'll have to sign of course, but you won't be allowed to keep a copy of that particular amendment. But it doesn't matter anyway. You're right, that specific clause would never hold up in a court of law. It doesn't have to."

Lara raised a perfectly sculpted eyebrow. "It doesn't?"

Stephen saved Tristan from trying to formulate an answer that wouldn't send her running out the door. "If we don't do what he says when he comes to collect, he kills us."

In almost a century of doing business this way, Tristan had seen many reactions to this part of his disclosure. He'd expected Lara to gasp, swoon, maybe even cry out in protest. She did none of those things. Instead, she met his gaze boldly. "Saints don't kill people who won't do as they command, Mr. Chance."

He found he didn't like the way she addressed him by his surname. He wanted intimacy between them, the kind that came with being familiar and comfortable enough with one another to use first names.

Damn.

The more time he spent around her, the more he came to realize that the attraction between them wasn't simply a physical reaction. There was something else that drew him to her, a bond that felt deeper, stronger and more compelling with every passing moment. It would have been so much simpler if he'd only wanted Lara for a night of sin, but she wasn't just a woman who could satisfy his needs, though he was certain she could do that too.

No, on a primal, instinctual level, whether she knew it or not, Lara was *his*.

"Perhaps that's because no one's dared turn down a direct request from a saint before, Lara." He deliberately chose not to use her family name in return and her eyes narrowed slightly in response.

"This is ridiculous." She ran a hand through her tightly bound hair, dislodging more strands from the neat bun. Disheveled black curls flew around her face. She looked innocent, almost pure, and the rush of heat coiling in his groin felt ripe with possibility.

He wouldn't delay any longer.

Tristan rose, removed three sheets of paper from the envelope and then placed one in front each member of the Montgomery family. Overhead, the bright neon lights flickered and dimmed momentarily.

Stephen signed first, though he wouldn't meet Tristan's eyes. Elias followed suit, slumping back in his seat afterward like a man who'd just signed his own death sentence.

Lara held the pen half an inch from the paper as he walked to stand behind her. Her hand shook and the same tremor ran through Tristan when he placed both palms on her shoulders.

She tensed at his touch, though she didn't jerk out of his grasp. "Why do I feel as though I'm about to sign my soul over to the Devil?"

Tristan shrugged. "If you'd prefer, think of it as something more pleasurable instead."

"Like what?"

He leaned over to whisper in her ear. "A cat and mouse game."

Chapter Three

೫೦

If someone had told Lara an hour ago she'd be ready to fall into bed with an arrogant, powerful man at the first suggestion, she'd have scoffed at the absurd idea. Men like her father didn't attract her. Their need to control, to flaunt their wealth, influence and dominance over everyone they came into contact with did nothing to turn her on.

She preferred the quiet type, men with more brains than brawn. In the four years she'd spent at Harvard, she'd met plenty and dated a few. They'd been decent enough in bed, she supposed, but none of the feelings they'd inspired came close to the pounding, needy ache thrumming through her body at the feel of Tristan's hand on her shoulder.

Trying hard to ignore the searing effect of his touch through the thick material of her suit jacket, Lara focused on the movement of her hand over the smooth surface of the table.

When she finished, the jagged edges of her signature on the dotted line stared back at her, black against the white paper, like a deep wound scored forever into the page. For a moment, regret prodded its way into her heart but she pushed it aside.

She'd made her decision, for better or for worse. Now she had to live with it.

If she lived long enough for it to matter.

Willing her hand not to tremble, she handed the form to Tristan without looking at him. "Just so you know, I only signed this because it's best for the business. It has nothing to do with you or with the stupid IOU."

"If that'll help you sleep at night, sweetheart, you go ahead and tell yourself that."

Son of a bitch.

She gritted her teeth. When she spoke, the words came out harsh and unforgiving. "If you ever come to collect on your absurd stipulation, just know I won't do it. You can ask for something as simple as a loaf of bread but you won't get it from me."

Beside her, Stephen tensed. "Maybe we didn't use words that were small enough for you to understand. This man has the ability to—"

"Snap me in half like a twig? Probably." She forced a calm she didn't feel into her voice and deliberately chose to ignore the slight. "But he can't bully me into doing his bidding."

"Ah, my altruistic moral-to-a-fault sister." Elias' contemptuous smile didn't quite reach his eyes. "You still haven't figured out how the world works, have you?"

"Enough. You can have your family squabbles when I'm gone." Tristan withdrew his hand and the loss of that connection almost made Lara gasp. Heat flooded her core, drenching her panties. She pressed her thighs together firmly, praying the incessant need would dissipate before she succumbed to the insane urge to rip her clothes off and really give her father something to be outraged about.

Her feelings made no sense. Blazing anger warred with intense arousal. How was it possible to hate someone and want him at the same time?

She almost smiled at that. Hadn't she both hated and loved her father her entire life?

Besides, she wasn't naïve enough to think she had to be in love to feel lust. Granted, it would be nice if she actually *liked* the men she was attracted to, but that hadn't always been the case. Despite what her brother believed, Lara knew too well how the world worked. Divorced parents and a dysfunctional home life didn't leave much room for romantic fantasies that ended happily ever after.

"The forms are all signed and that's all that matters. Deal's done." She heard the sound of shuffling papers as Tristan stuffed the forms back inside the envelope. "My lawyers will be in touch with you."

That's it? He's leaving?

Her pounding heartbeat almost drowned out her father's strained words as he made some polite suggestion or other. Tristan didn't answer. He rounded the long table and headed for the door.

Before Lara could consider her actions, she was on her feet and running after him. "Wait."

He didn't even slow his stride until he reached the elevators and pushed the button then rounded on her. "What is it?"

The sensual awareness between them sizzled with electricity. For a brief moment Lara thought that if she squinted, she'd actually be able to see sparks flickering in the brief space separating their bodies.

"I..."

Tristan's deep green eyes bore into hers with an intensity that made her mouth go dry. She shook her head and tried again. "I wanted to apologize for my family. We're not exactly the Brady Bunch."

A deep growl echoed from his throat, primal and unforgiving. She blinked and in that instant his hand was in the air, so fast she hadn't even seen him move. Her heart pounded hard against her rib cage. The realization that he was going to hit her slammed into her through a dazed fog of perception.

She flinched when his hand made contact but the touch was impossibly gentle, a soft caress that sent a shudder down her spine. A moan slipped out between her lips before she could stop it.

He leaned in, his mouth only inches away from hers. His expression was dark as an oncoming thunderstorm. "Why do you let them talk to you like that?"

She licked her lips. Shame flooded her cheeks and she averted her gaze, focusing instead on the metallic sheen of the elevator doors behind him. "I don't expect you to understand. They're...family."

"I have family too. My brothers would never dare question me." She heard no boasting in his tone, only concern mingled with dismay.

"Sure. It's easy to obey a guy who threatens to kill people who don't do as he commands."

Emotions flickered over Tristan's face but were gone before she could discern them. "I don't always use my power to get what I want."

Lara pressed her lips together, afraid another strangled groan might escape before she could stop it. The sexy innuendo hung between them as the silence stretched on. All she had to do was reach out and grab it—grab *him*—and bring his mouth down an additional inch. Then she could taste him, slip her tongue inside his mouth and give in to the temptation that had been plaguing her incessantly for two days.

The elevator bell announced its arrival with a ding that echoed loudly in the empty hall. She took a step back, breaking the invisible connection between them. She splayed her palm over her stomach to soothe the butterflies that had settled there.

Even Tristan's usual mask of perfect self-control seemed shaken by what had almost happened between them. His gaze swept her face, settling on her lips. She fought the urge to lick them.

"Let me drive you home," Tristan suggested. The husky invitation sent a jolt of heat to her pussy. Arousal slicked her folds, tightened her nipples. It would be so easy to give in, to say yes and step into the elevator without looking back.

Lara shook her head. "Thanks, but no. I'll take a cab."

As soon as the words left her mouth, she wanted to take them back, to pretend she'd never spoken them. The sensual spell hovering in the air snapped and broke for good.

Tristan inclined his head. "Suit yourself," he said, stepping backward into the gaping maw of the elevator. Lara watched as he disappeared behind the sliding double doors, her muscles clenched tightly in silent protest.

She returned to the boardroom slowly, her legs trembling with every step. What would it have been like to make love to Tristan Chance? The man radiated the need to control—it drove every move he made. That same deeply seeded desire would also be behind his actions in the bedroom. He'd want to dominate, to take charge of every sensual act.

He probably owned entire sets of handcuffs, whips, paddles. He'd ask her to wear stilettos and a school-girl outfit, and she'd be forced to obey his every command until she was drenched in his pleasure, sticky with his cum.

The thought should have repulsed her, should have sent her fleeing for the safely of her small apartment, but it had the opposite effect. Her breasts felt heavy, ripe with need. Wet heat had formed into a puddle, soaking the crotch of her panties. She could smell her own ravenous arousal and the realization terrified her.

What was it about Tristan Chance that drew her like a magnet? Every time he came near, she had the ridiculous notion that his soul called out to hers, making it impossible for her to say no.

But she had said no.

It had taken all her willpower to deny his sensual request but she'd done it. If she had to, she could do it again.

And he would ask again, of that she was certain. A man who wielded his personal power like a weapon wouldn't take no for an answer. Would he use his IOU clause to fuck her, if he wanted her bad enough?

Would she be disappointed if he didn't?

Anticipation zinged through Lara's bloodstream. She clenched her teeth, promising herself once again she'd say no if he asked, no matter how much his emerald eyes shone with barely contained lust. She wasn't going to let a piece of paper dictate her life, nor would she let Tristan push her around by sheer force of will. Two overbearing men in her life were almost more than she could handle. She didn't want another.

Heated whispers echoed into the hallway and she hesitated just outside the boardroom.

"You know what has to be done." Elias' voice shook with barely contained anger. He punctuated his words with rhythmic slams of his fist against the table.

"You're sure the information you've received is accurate?" Stephen asked.

"Absolutely. Tristan Chance might look like the powerful businessman he wants everyone to believe he is, but in truth, he's a fierce, dangerous creature who must be stopped at any cost."

Lara's heartbeat quickened. She pressed herself against the wall, straining to hear more.

"I've run many business deals in my day, son. But never have I had to deal with a..." He uttered the next word too low for Lara to hear. She gritted her teeth, frustration and a hint of uneasiness sliding down her spine.

"And that's exactly why you must call the Sanctuary immediately. They'll know what to do."

Stephen sighed. "At what cost?"

"Money's no longer an object. Besides, this is too important."

"What about Lara?"

"What about her? If the slut wants to offer herself on a sacrificial platter, I say let her —"

She'd heard enough. Lifting her chin, her pulse thundering in her temples, she strode into the boardroom. Avoiding the fierce glares her brother and father threw her way, she picked up her briefcase.

"He seems to have taken quite an interest in you."

She gritted her teeth, determined not to get into this discussion with her father. He and Elias had already made up their mind about her. "I'm not even going to try to dignify that with an answer. Good night, Dad."

"No, really, Lara. The man has a point." Elias' easy confidence had returned, Lara noted, wishing Tristan had stayed just a little while longer so her brother could have sniveled for another few minutes. Some much-needed humility certainly wouldn't hurt him.

Neither would a healthy dose of skin-drenching fear.

"And what point are you making exactly, Dad?" Lara slammed the briefcase onto the table and whirled around to face them both. "If you're trying to come up with a snide remark about my clothes, my hair, my body or anything else meant to disparage me, go right ahead. I've heard it all before and believe it or not, it doesn't bother me anymore."

She'd been doing well until that last part, Lara thought, trying to hide a grimace. At least she'd kept her tone steady and hadn't broken eye contact. A small victory, but she had to take them where she could get them these days.

Stephen waved a hand in the air and Lara gritted her teeth, feeling a vein in her jaw begin to throb. He could dismiss her concerns without even having to speak and that irked her more than a mean-spirited comment would have.

"Like it or not, you're an easy target," Elias continued. "We can't have Chance sniffing around our doorstep whenever his cock gets hard."

An image flashed before Lara's eyes. Tristan leaning against the doorframe, naked and aroused, his lean muscles rippling with desperate need, a devastatingly seductive grin on his exquisite features. She shook her head to clear the ill-timed thought but it was too late. Her face had already heated in response to the vivid fantasy and her father's brows pulled downward in a frown Lara knew too well.

"You're leaving New York."

She quirked an eyebrow, the only outward manifestation of surprise she'd allow herself. "Like hell I am."

"This isn't a discussion, Lara. Your plane tickets are being booked as we speak."

"And just where exactly am I going?"

"Away from Tristan Chance," Elias supplied, his perfect row of white teeth gleaming in the harsh neon light.

Lara's stomach churned. Bile rose in her throat as a wave of dizziness washed over her. She propped her hip against the edge of the long table to keep from teetering on her two-inch pumps. "Tristan isn't interested in me," she said, as much to convince herself as her father.

Stephen narrowed his eyes and pursed his lips in quiet concentration. "Maybe not. He probably has a dozen floozies at his beck and call, but that's a risk I'm not willing to take. You're going to Florida to supervise the first of our renovation projects."

"Why Florida?"

Stephen shrugged. "It's as good a spot as any. The profit reports from that area haven't been positive. We've considered shutting down the hotel but perhaps it's the best place to start renovating."

"And you want me to oversee this entire undertaking?" She frowned, the sparks of excitement mingling with doubt and confusion in her mind.

This all sounded much too good to be true. After all these years, could her father finally have come to terms with everything she could offer the company? He was giving her a chance to prove herself, and if that wasn't incredible enough, he was also allowing her to do it far away from him.

She'd maintain her independence while proving her self-worth. The myriad possibilities that swam through her mind made her head pound. "What's the catch?"

"You're not to have any further contact with Tristan Chance."

A trail of fire and ice slid over her skin at the mere mention of Tristan's name. She hid a shiver as best she could. "I don't think he's going to follow me to Florida, Dad."

Stephen nodded. "Probably not. Just the same, if he comes after you, do everything in your power to stay away from him. If that means flying halfway around the world, do it."

A million protests hovered on the tip of Lara's tongue but she swallowed them back. "Not to worry. Unless he comes calling to collect his IOU, I doubt I'll be seeing him again."

"Good. Make sure you remember that. The man is danger."

Her laugh sounded hollow even to her own ears. "You mean he's dangerous."

Stephen shrugged. "He reeks of danger. I don't want you anywhere near him."

When had her father begun to care about her welfare? The foreign concern in his voice unnerved her until she realized it was probably just one more way for him to make sure he remained in control.

She picked up her briefcase and with a wave of her hand over her shoulder, swept through the door. In the elevator, she glanced in the mirror only long enough to note her disheveled hair, her too-bright eyes. Fierce excitement blazed in her veins.

She'd finally have everything she wanted. Respect. Trust.

Independence.

The elevator doors slid open and she resisted the urge to skip through the marble foyer. "'Night, Michael!" she called out to the security guard.

"Do you need a cab, Ms. Montgomery?"

"It's a beautiful night. I think I'll walk."

"Be careful out there, miss."

She dismissed his concerns with a slight incline of her head and breezed through the revolving doors. The cool December air wrapped her in its crisp winter scent and she inhaled deeply, relishing the New York City night. All around her holiday lights shone like strings of jewels draped around window frames, doorways and strung in trees.

Lara would miss her hometown, but the idea of wearing a bikini on Christmas day held its own brand of appeal. She turned right on Third Ave East, following the line of the subway rattling the ground beneath her feet. The distant red and blue glow of the Empire State Building guided her steps toward her apartment building.

Cabs zoomed by at top speed but she didn't bother to flag one. It would only take half an hour to get home and the cold air felt heavenly on her overheated skin. A prickle of awareness hinted that her raised temperature had little to do with her upcoming trip but she pushed that thought to the dark edges of her mind.

She'd only walked half a block when a stretch limousine pulled up beside her. Midnight black and glistening in the pools of light cast by the streetlamps, the vehicle was impossible to ignore. Still, heart hammering hard against her rib cage, she did her best to pretend it wasn't there.

The mechanical whirr of a window being lowered made her quicken her pace. The car matched her speed.

"Lara."

God, how she loved her name on his lips. And how unfair that one word was all it took to unravel her self-control.

Her breath steamed the cold air. "I didn't think you'd collect on your precious clause so soon."

"I'm not here to make you do anything you don't want to do."

Her eyelids fluttered shut as his words sank in. Of all the things he could have said, that was the last statement she'd expected to hear from him. "I have trouble believing that."

"Then get in the car and let me show you."

She took a step toward the limo then another. There were a million reasons she shouldn't be doing this. Her career. Her father's wishes. Everything she'd worked so hard to achieve.

She tried to rationalize her decision as she walked around the car to the door he'd pushed open for her. It was her last night in New York. She'd never have to see him again. She hadn't *technically* promised her father she'd stay away from Tristan and besides, Stephen would never know.

Sliding in the backseat, Lara sank into the leather upholstery. A flutter of fear and anticipation churned in her stomach. Despite all the excuses, there was only one reason strong enough to have propelled her the extra step.

She wanted to.

* * * * *

The sound of the door slamming closed behind Lara echoed with an eerie sense of finality through the limo. She sat on the long bench opposite Tristan and crossed a long leg over the other, drawing his gaze to what little he could see of the inside of her thigh.

Tristan pushed a small black button on a sleek panel anchored to the door closest to him and the car drew away from the curb. "I thought you said you'd take cab home."

She shrugged, not quite meeting his gaze. "It's a nice night."

He lifted an eyebrow. "It's cold as hell and you're not wearing a coat."

"Great. Now you're going to give me a lecture on my wardrobe too? This is ridiculous." She reached for the door handle then stopped abruptly. "Where are we going?"

"Tom's well trained. He'll drive around for a while until I instruct him where to go. And for the record, no, I'm not telling you what you should wear. If you enjoy turning into an icicle, be my guest. What really concerns me is that you don't see anything wrong with taking a leisurely stroll through Manhattan's Upper East Side at two in the morning."

She shuddered visibly as the full meaning of his words sank in. "I'm a New Yorker. I know these streets as well as I know my own apartment. I didn't think..." Light flooded her face as they passed under a streetlight. She looked up at him, her dark gaze assessing, questioning. "You followed me." It wasn't a question.

Tristan shook his head. "Actually, no. I should have but I thought the doorman would get you a cab. There's certainly no shortage of those in this city." He forced a lightness he didn't feel into his voice but his stomach churned. He'd left the Montgomery Suites building half an hour ago, his cock aching after Lara's rejection.

He'd intended to go straight home but less than five minutes after leaving the building, the limo slid to a stop. A police roadblock, Tom had told him. NY's finest were looking for a fugitive and they were checking every car that crossed their path then rerouting traffic away from the blazing scene of a violent crime. A man had set a woman's car on fire...with her still in it.

He shook his head. "Gotta love New York."

Lara smiled wistfully. "It's home, for better or worse." She met his gaze, her features still guarded. "So if you didn't follow me, how did you know exactly where to find me?"

That was the million-dollar question, wasn't it? He hadn't gone after her as perhaps he should have, yet when he'd spotted her strolling along the darkened sidewalk, he'd recognized her instantly. Once again, she'd been drawn into his path—or he'd been pulled into hers. Did it even matter?

The only explanation that made any sense, no matter how warped, was that the family curse Hayden had gone on about for centuries had finally found him.

Of course, this could still be pure coincidence. After all, it wasn't as though he'd run into her in a completely unexpected place. She'd been only a couple of blocks away from the Montgomery Suites building.

"Thank New York's finest." He told Lara about the roadblock and the rerouted traffic then held his breath as she pondered his revelations.

"So you really didn't come after me on purpose?"

Was that disappointment he heard in her voice? He wished he could read her mind but he hadn't had so much as a glimmer of her inner thoughts since she'd climbed into the car.

"I—"

"Forget it." She held up a hand. "I don't really want to know." She blew out a long breath then ran a hand through her hair. Messy strands flew wildly around her head and she yanked on the clip holding her tresses together. Long black curls spilled over her shoulders, a startling contrast to her pale skin. He'd thought her beautiful when he'd first seen her, but now he realized how wrong he'd been. She wasn't simply beautiful—she was stunning, an exotic wonder his for the taking.

A jolt of pure, animal need rushed straight into Tristan's cock, pounding hard against his shaft as it stiffened. Lara nibbled her lower lip and stared at him from beneath lowered eyelashes. The sounds of the city faded into the distance as the tension between them mounted, filling the air with the sparks of crackling energy.

Unable to hold back any longer, Tristan lunged from his seat. He knew she wouldn't see him move, and when he pressed his body against hers, he captured her startled cry inside his mouth.

Fisting her hands in his suit jacket, Lara's body went rigid. He waited while the inner battle raged inside her, his mouth clamped against hers, his tongue sweeping gently over her full lips.

As soon as her tense muscles slackened and her lush curves molded to his body, Tristan buried his tongue inside her mouth. She tasted of mint, a flavor he'd never found particularly arousing but that he now couldn't get enough of. Their tongues met in a slow, sensual caress—searching, savoring, exploring.

Her full breasts pressed against him as she kissed him back just as fiercely, the softness of her body compounding the incessant need hammering into his groin. He could hear the rush of her blood streaming through her veins, the rapid rhythmic beat of her heart. It all conspired to make him lose control. His balls drew up, pulsing with a needy, familiar ache that signaled he was close to spilling his seed.

At the last moment he drew back, his labored breathing matching hers. He hadn't noticed his fangs extending but they had, and he raked them down the sensitive flesh of her throat, careful not to break the skin.

Hunger mingled with arousal, threatening to drive him into a frenzy. He closed his eyes and forced some semblance of control into his enflamed body then took her hand and guided it to the stiff erection tenting his pants.

When he spoke, his hoarse voice sounded foreign to his ears. "See what you do to me?"

"I'm flattered," Lara murmured, her palm skimming over his hard length. "But I doubt I'm doing anything a thousand other women haven't done before."

He chuckled against her shoulder as he unbuttoned her jacket and slid his hands up along her rib cage to cup both breasts. He circled her nipples with his thumbs, eliciting a carnal moan in response.

"It hasn't quite been that many."

"Hundreds then," she amended playfully. Her breath fanned his cheek, the sweet smell of mint sending an icy path straight to his cock.

A moment later she had his fly undone. Her fingers crept inside the easy-access slit of his boxers, sliding over his pulsing dick with slow, expert movements. "Your skin is so cold," she whispered, the tip of her nail grazing the engorged head of his cock.

He trailed a finger along the valley between her inner thighs and she wriggled as she spread her legs, giving him full access to the place he'd been yearning to touch since he'd met her.

That night, her pussy had been fully covered by a strategic array of lettuce leaves and pineapple slices. Now, the only thing standing between him and the juicy delicacy waiting at the apex of her thighs was a thin strip of silk. When he touched it, the material clung to her folds, soaked through with her arousal.

He slid the panties aside, dipping his middle finger inside the fragrant, moist heat. "Oh baby, you're hot enough for both of us."

"See what you do to me?" She repeated his words in a low, throaty voice while she pulled his cock through the gaping slit in his boxers. She wrapped her hand around his length and stroked him slowly, making small circular movements as she neared the tip of his shaft. Her palm slid over the oozing pre-cum dripping from his dick and she spread the slick moisture over his length, lubricating her strokes.

"Lift your legs," he commanded, and she obeyed without a hint of hesitation. She propped her heels on the edge of the wide leather bench, giving him as much access to her cunt as he needed. Her skirt slid up around her hips and he pushed her panties completely to one side, baring her shaved pussy and her full, pink labia to his gaze.

Her hand never left his cock. They sat side by side, she with her head propped against the headrest, he twisted slightly toward her so he could reach between her legs and play inside her dripping cunt.

"I'm going to shove my fingers inside you," he whispered in her ear. "Then after you've come, I'm going to replace my hand with my cock and I'm going to ask you which you prefer. If you have a problem with any of this, tell me now because, so help me God, I'm not going to stop once I really get started."

Lara whimpered in response, her grip tightening on his shaft. She squeezed his stiff length harder and increased her tempo. "Not if I make you come first."

"A challenge then." He found the entrance to her channel and nudged it, feeling the muscles gape at his insistent probing.

Lara dipped her fingers beneath the soft cotton of his boxers and cupped his balls, the sensation sending a tremor through his body. "You're on."

He slid two fingers inside her body slowly, gently, at first, waiting for her pussy to adjust to the intrusion. Meanwhile, she had no such compulsions about gentleness. Her hand worked at his cock with quick, rapid movements. Just the right speed, her motions were perfect, as though she'd practiced on his shaft her entire life. A flash of jealousy spread through his bloodstream. She hadn't been practicing on him, but it was clear that she *had* been practicing.

He thrust inside her harder, as though to punish her for the direction his thoughts had taken. Instead of protesting, Lara moaned while her pussy gripped him in its tight, inviting grip. His cock hardened farther until the ache in his balls became a driving, all-consuming need. He wanted to spill himself in her hand, to watch as his cum spurted from his cock and dripped over her blood-red nails.

But he wouldn't.

Tristan gritted his teeth and fought for the self-control he knew he possessed. Losing control was never an option. Not in his business and not in his personal life.

His thumb found the hard nub of Lara's clit and circled it, pressing down slightly when a small mewling sound escaped her throat. She squirmed against him as cream dripped down his fingers. Her breathing grew labored, coming in harsh gasps. The muscles in her thighs were corded as she moved her hips up to meet his hand.

"Don't hold back, baby," he urged her. "Come!"

She increased the pressure on his cock, her fingers flying over his length, her eyelids squeezed tight. "No." The word was no more than another gasp. "You'll win."

The determination in her voice started him. Of course he'd win. Had there ever been any doubt? That was the game, wasn't it?

Though her touch ignited a burning need deep within his core, he knew she was right on the brink of release and he intended to push her over the edge and watch as she tumbled straight into his arms.

But he hadn't counted on how much sway her rapid strokes could have on his needy cock. As his excitement grew, so did his hunger. Her heart pounded faster and faster the closer she came to climax, and his fangs lengthened to their full extent.

"You're mine, Lara. You're meant to be mine," he whispered.

He inched his head closer to her throat, his gaze fixed on the pulsing vein carrying so much sweet, mouthwatering blood. He needed to taste her, to have her essence flood his mouth just as her cream flooded his hand.

The need to sample her unique flavor consumed him. It thundered in his temples and made his mouth water. His fangs ached with the desire to feel her flesh give way as he pierced the tender skin of her throat. His head spun, all thoughts centered on the heated rhythm of her blood flowing just beneath the surface of her alabaster skin.

Wanting her flavor on his tongue was more than a craving. It was a dark, deep, desperate necessity akin to a diabetic's need for insulin. If he didn't obtain approximately twelve fluid ounces in a twenty-four hour period, his powers would drain quickly, as would his life force. A ravenous vampire became ruthless, ruled by the simple need to feed.

Tristan refused to allow himself to be driven by his hunger. He knew he had to take her, yet this sudden compulsion ran deeper than that simple need for sustenance.

With a groan, his restraint flew into the dark recesses of his mind, bringing out the primal, predatory part of him. He sank his fangs in her neck in one smooth motion at the same time the limo came to an abrupt stop, tires squealing on the pavement. Lara cried out and her hips pitched forward at the brisk halting motion, embedding Tristan's fingers deeper into her pulsing pussy. His thumb pushed harder against her clit.

Oh God, no! No, I won't! I… Oh God!

She came with deep, shuddering moans that could have been sobs as her protests rang through his mind. Her sweet, coppery blood spilled into his mouth and gushed down his throat while her cum flooded his hand to drip onto the leather bench.

Her climax set off his own and his hips bucked upward as cum spurted from his cock in a hot, sticky torrent. His balls contracted and his shaft trembled while he spent himself in wave after wave of delicious agony.

As he pumped out the last of his cum and Lara's orgasm subsided, he reluctantly pulled his fangs from her neck. He'd only been able to obtain about half the amount of blood he required, but he didn't dare risk feeding from her any longer than necessary as she recovered from the tremors of climax.

The limo had begun to move again, picking up speed. He wondered how far away they were from his mansion.

Lapping at the last drops of blood trickling from the wounds, he shuddered as her thoughts of protest quieted and silence replaced her throaty voice in his head. He watched as his healing saliva drew the puncture wounds closed until they resembled no more than two small burgundy marks.

He placed a soft kiss over the wounds he'd inflicted, knowing she wouldn't remember how she'd come to have them. Women were easiest to feed from because once on the brink of orgasm, the brief pain of a vampire bite didn't even register on their distress meter.

"Come home with me tonight," he whispered.

Lara's body went rigid. Or rather, he realized belatedly, her muscles hadn't relaxed after her strenuous release. When she turned her head to look at him, her dark eyes glistened wildly. She stared blankly, as though she didn't recognize him, then pulled back and flung herself to the opposite bench.

"I need to get out of here." The desperation in her voice cut straight through his post-orgasmic afterglow.

"I'll tell Tom to drive you home," he said, reaching for her.

"No!" she screamed, batting his hand away. Her hair flew in disarray around her shoulders as she shook her head. "I need to get out *now*." Her hand closed around the door handle.

Tristan banged on the divider separating the back seat from the driver's compartment. "Tom! Stop the car!"

The limo swerved wildly to the right then came to a halting stop. Lara yanked the handle of her briefcase, smoothed her skirt down over her thighs and flew from the car right into traffic.

Tristan swore loudly and leapt out after her. A loud horn blared and a semi truck zoomed past his field of vision, flattening him against the limo. His heart pounded wildly, fear zinging through his veins.

He couldn't see Lara.

Desperate to make his way across the four-lane road, he held up both hands in front of moving vehicles and took off at a run. A moment later he caught a glimpse of Lara's bare leg as she swung it inside the backseat of a cab. She didn't look his way as she slammed the door closed. The bright yellow taxi drove away in the opposite direction, leaving him standing in the middle of a busy lane while frustrated drivers leaned on their horns.

He was already punching in numbers on his cell phone as he returned to the limo. Tom, a short, stocky man who had been with him for almost two decades, leaned out the window and looked out in concern. Tristan waved him back and then slid into the warm bench, pulling the door shut behind him.

The limo smelled of sex and mint. Warm air from a nearby heating vent rushed over his skin, warming his cock.

He looked down at his now soft dick and slammed his fist against the window. It rattled but held.

Fan-fucking-tastic.

Tristan gritted his teeth. Anger cleared his mind of the aching dread that had gripped him since he'd watched Lara run out from the limo.

This was just fucking perfect. Frantic about Lara, he'd run out into traffic with his zipper open, his cock flapping in the breeze, sticky cum staining his pants. That was just the professional, authoritative image he wanted to present.

"Hello?" The voice on the other end of the line raised his spirits a little and Tristan smiled despite himself.

"I need your help, little brother."

Hayden's warm laugh slid through the telephone line. "If Hell had frozen over, I'd have heard about it on the weather channel."

"Then make sure you keep the TV turned on." Tristan ran a hand through his unbound hair. "Tell me, this curse of yours...it wouldn't happen to make women run away screaming, would it?"

The lightness disappeared from Hayden's tone. "Only if you happen to be the direct cause of an orgasm." He paused, as though considering his next words. "You've never believed in the family curse before. Something's happened."

Tristan blew out a deep breath, remembering the way Lara had looked at him right before she bolted. As though she feared him more than she feared three thousand pounds of metal coming at her at sixty miles an hour.

"I think I better come see you. We need to talk."

"You know you're always welcome here. But if you've found your soul mate—"

"I'll tell you everything," Tristan promised. "Later."

Not quite ready to contemplate the whole soul mate scenario, he wasn't going to let Hayden go off on another rant about the curse. It was bad enough he'd begun taking this nonsense seriously. For three centuries, he'd vehemently denied Hayden's claims that men in their family had been cursed to run into their soul mates at odd times in unexpected places, doomed to never keep the women by their side.

Nonsense, all of it. And yet…

Tristan shuddered, refusing to let his mind linger on the fact that Lara would rather leap from a vehicle in the middle of a busy street than spend another moment with him.

He'd listen to what Hayden had to say, and if any of it made sense, he'd figure out his next move then. Meanwhile, it would be good to see his brother.

"As you wish, but this is important," Hayden said. "When will you be arriving?"

"I'll have the jet readied for take off immediately."

"Good. Delaying at this point would only make things worse."

Tristan rolled his eyes, preparing to hang up when Hayden spoke again. "Oh and leave the heavy suits at home this time, okay? Wear something more suitable."

"Like what?"

"Like, I don't know…a Hawaiian shirt? It's hot in the Florida Keys this time of year."

Chuckling, Tristan thanked his brother for the advice and snapped his cell phone shut. His closet probably held a couple of pairs of jeans and a few T-shirts but anything even slightly resembling Hawaiian print definitely wouldn't exist anywhere in his home. Unlike Hayden, who'd made his wealth designing a successful men's clothing line and running a wildly popular chain of men's clothing stores, Tristan's wardrobe consisted of three dozen suits, in four different colors. That covered all his basic needs and suited every season. Even the heat of the Florida Keys.

He pressed the red button twice, instructing Tom to drive home. Glittering city lights flickered against the navy blue sky. A ribbon of pale pink streaked the horizon, announcing the rapidly approaching dawn.

Lara's wild eyes blazed on the inside of Tristan's eyelids as he closed his eyes. He hadn't even had a chance to fulfill his promise. He'd wanted to fill her with his cock, to watch her lips as she moaned in ecstasy while he thrust into her hot, willing cunt.

He'd go to Florida and listen to Hayden's wild beliefs. It was worth the trip just to dismiss the silly curse as the cause of Lara's frenzied distress.

And when he returned, he'd make sure she never ran away from him again.

Chapter Four

ഇ

Lara clenched her teeth until her jaw hurt. She pressed the button to the fifteenth floor while a reworked instrumental version of some popular pop song streamed from the ceiling and flooded the elevator.

"Merry Christmas!" The woman's cheery voice seemed to demand an answer but Lara ignored her, carefully avoiding making eye contact. She didn't know many of her neighbors but she remembered this one as always wearing some flamboyant color. Tonight she'd picked a short fuchsia miniskirt and matching top. The colors blazed in Lara's peripheral vision.

"Did you get all your shopping done?"

Lara groaned. Why did people insist on talking in the elevator? This woman had to be from out of state. In New York, that kind of upbeat conversation with a stranger could get a person killed.

"It's not Christmas yet," Lara managed to say through the tears forming a lump in her throat. "And it's almost five in the morning."

"The city never sleeps," the neighbor singsonged.

Lara watched the red electronic readout above the doors flicker to fourteen then fifteen. A sigh of relief escaped her lips as she slid through the doors the moment they began to open.

"Good night!" the neighbor called after her, but Lara didn't stop to reciprocate the sentiment.

The heel of her right pump twisted as she ran down the hall. Kicking it off, she watched it slam against her apartment door. She shoved her key into the lock with trembling fingers then pushed the shoe inside with her bare foot.

Only when she'd driven the deadbolt home did Lara stop to flick on the overhead light. The bright illumination seemed to summon forth all the tears she'd been fighting back and they spilled down her cheeks in an unheeded stream.

Lara slumped against the wall and slid to the ground. Her stomach lurched.

What had gotten into her? One moment she was having the most incredible orgasm of her life and the next she was wild with fear, her heart threatening to shatter her breastbone with its incessant pounding. The need to get away from Tristan had suddenly been so deep, so primal, it felt as though her life had depended on it.

At that moment she'd known for certain that if she didn't take her chances with the oncoming traffic, she'd be dead.

Lara drew her knees up to her chest and wrapped her arms around them, rocking back and forth. The terror had subsided but frenzied confusion took its place as she tried to make sense of what she'd done.

She remembered getting into the limo despite her father's warnings. Was this what her irrational fear had been all about? Had Stephen and Elias' trepidation about the man who had just saved their business somehow transferred to Lara, making her lose control of her emotions?

She'd heard of people doing some strange things at the pinnacle of climax but she'd never heard of anything quite like this.

Rising on shaky legs, she reached out to steady herself and wrapped her fingers around the skinny neck of the oriental vase she kept by the front door. When it started wobbling on its narrow base, she released it, watching as it righted itself. Of all the pieces in her eclectic collection of knickknacks, the vase was her favorite.

She ran her fingers over the delicate mosaic pattern running down its length and sighed. One day she'd be able to afford the entire set. There were twelve vases in total but it had taken half her savings just to afford this one. If only her father would actually treat her as the heir to his empire rather than just a lowly employee, she'd quickly be able to acquire the rest of the vases.

Heading for the bathroom, Lara shook her head, annoyed at herself. It wasn't as though the business had been doing well anyway.

Yet she knew Elias made much more money than she did. Then again, Elias had always been his father's favorite child while Lara had been nothing but a constant disappointment. It was worse when they'd all lived under one roof. Stephen had made it clear as soon as she hit puberty that he expected Lara to marry into a wealthy family and produce a litter of offspring as quickly as possible. She, on the other hand, had wanted a career of her own. More importantly though, she'd wanted independence.

In the end, she'd gotten it. The day she received her acceptance letter from Harvard was both the best and the worst of her life. Holding the papers in her hand, she'd actually allowed herself to think that she would not only gain her freedom but also her father's respect. He'd have no choice but to realize she'd grown into a responsible adult who no longer had to obey his every parental whim.

What a fool she'd been.

Instead of pride, contempt had blazed in Stephen's gaze. She could still recall the burning shame, the angry tears streaming down her cheeks as he'd crumpled the letter and tossed it into the trash.

She'd fished it out from among a banana peel and a can of tuna, drying her eyes with her sleeve. After she'd smoothed the wrinkles with a tight fist, she filled out the forms.

Two part-time jobs and four years later, she'd returned home, degree in hand. That driving desire to please her father had been behind every scholarship she received, every perfect grade. She hadn't expected a warm homecoming but she'd hoped that if she showed him what she could do for Montgomery Suites, he'd have no choice but to admit he was wrong. That hadn't happened.

Until tonight.

The cold tile sent a chill into Lara's bare feet. She flicked the light switch, flooding the room in harsh neon light, then ran the hot water inside the small tub. She needed a bath, as much to calm her ruffled nerves as to wash away the memory of Tristan's hands on her body.

Tonight she'd experienced a once-in-a-lifetime kind of lapse in judgment. She'd been warned to stay away from Tristan, yet she hadn't listened and she'd almost ended up with her insides splattered across the pavement for her efforts.

Granted, she'd also ended up with a mind-blowing orgasm but that seemed like a distant memory now.

Heat swirled inside her, settling low in her stomach and then sliding lower still. Her pussy pulsed in obvious disagreement. She could still feel Tristan's hands on her, gentle at first then increasingly insistent as she denied him—and herself—the release they both craved.

Exhaustion crept in, nudging Lara's eyelids, but she knew she wouldn't be able to sleep until she scrubbed off the scent of her arousal, the sticky cum now dry on her inner thigh.

She needed a good night's sleep, that was all. Tomorrow she'd start fresh, far away from Tristan Chance and his irresistible touch.

She stripped quickly, tossing her clothes in a corner of the room. The skirt came off last and as she heaped it on top of the pile, she noticed a white, telling stain. It would wash out, she assured herself, her cunt muscles tightening in recognition.

And if it didn't, she'd burn the entire suit.

Water rippled around Lara's knees as she stepped inside the tub, the warmth of it stoking the fire burning inside her cunt. She pressed her thighs together and lowered herself into the bath. The water barely reached her chest. It lapped at her nipples and the traitorous buds perked, so sensitive she drew in a sharp breath as air slid across the wet flesh, making her shiver.

She cupped her breasts, letting the weight of them linger in her hands. Tristan had touched her this way. If she closed her eyes, she could still feel his caress, her body soaking in the burning heat from the contact.

No. She couldn't think this way. She had to get Tristan out of her system for good.

Dunking her head under the water to clear it, she thought about how odd it was that his skin had felt so cold and yet his touch had instantly lit a fire throughout every inch of her body. It made no sense but then, nothing did anymore. Not the way she felt around him. Not her father's sudden trust in her.

Nothing.

She came up for air and slicked her hair back, desperately trying not to give in to the fire burning inside her cunt. It felt as though he'd left a part of himself there, stroking her to arousal each time she thought of him. Her clit throbbed and she wiggled, her ass sliding on the slick surface of the tub.

This was ridiculous. She had to assuage the ache between her legs or she definitely wouldn't get any sleep.

Reluctantly she gave in, her thumb and forefinger latching on a nipple. She'd wanted Tristan to do the same thing and she knew he would have, had she agreed to his invitation to go home with him.

Tweaking the hard bud, she thought about his teeth clamped on her breast, digging into her flesh. Pain built and traveled through her nerve endings, lighting an overheated path straight to her sex.

She lowered the washcloth over her stomach, dipping it into the water and cupping her smooth mound in her palm through the soft material. She applied pressure gently, slowly pulsing her fingers against her clit.

Her moan echoed through the empty room. She licked her lips, remembering the feel of Tristan's hard cock in her hand, his sensual groans as she stroked him faster, harder, with more urgency than she'd thought herself capable of.

She'd needed his cum as much as he'd needed hers. Her soul had cried out for his pleasure while the logical part of her brain fought for control. She'd known even then, in that desperate, lust-filled fog, that coming first would mean giving herself to him body and soul. She couldn't bear that.

No man would ever control her again, not even one who knew just how to send her over the edge with a flick of his expert fingertips.

But, God, how she'd ached to bring her lips down on his thick, hard cock, to warm the icy-cold shaft with her tongue. He'd have come then, inside her eager mouth. She knew it just as she knew she needed air to breathe. It would have been easy to win his little challenge and still, she hadn't been able to move. Her hips had thrust upward of their own accord, meeting his every thrust. If she'd changed positions, he'd no longer have had such easy access to her pussy and the overwhelming intensity of his caress would have left her without the satisfaction her body craved.

Pulsing need throbbed, pounded and rippled, grazing her skin, tightening her muscles. She tossed the washcloth aside and spread her legs, thrusting two fingers inside the entrance to her slick pussy. They slid in easily, her cream lubricating her tight channel and making room for the intrusion. She pumped her fingers in and out of her cunt just as he'd done, her thumb grazing her clit with each thrust.

She hovered on the edge, her pussy quivering as she held back, gritting her teeth. She'd wanted to forget about Tristan tonight but she'd accomplished the opposite. Determined not to come again with Tristan's face etched upon her mind, she tried to conjure up other men's features.

Celebrities, men from work, it didn't mater. Their faces flashed into existence briefly but they all morphed into *him*.

Don't think. Just don't fucking think!

Strong jaw. Full lips. And a brooding green gaze that sent a jolt straight to her cunt.

Images of Tristan touching every inch of her body flooded Lara's thoughts. The delicate flesh at the side of her neck throbbed with a dull, barely remembered ache. Then her climax exploded, wrenching a cry from her throat.

Sensation rushed through her body, causing her to shudder with desperate spasms that shook her to her very core.

You're mine, Lara. You're meant to be mine.

She thrashed, splashing lukewarm water everywhere. Her sensitive skin and still-spasming muscles protested not being allowed to recover naturally but she had to know if he was here—if she'd really heard his voice or if she was actually going insane.

"Hello?" She peered intently into every corner of her small bathroom but the room remained just as empty as it had been a moment before. Yet she'd heard his words as clearly as she'd heard them in the limo when he'd whispered in her ear.

Great. As if the incessant lust and her body's consuming need for him wasn't enough.

The rippling water engulfing her soaked into Lara's skin, pressing against her from all sides. Suddenly, what should have been a comforting weight became too much to bear. She rose and stepped out of the tub, reaching for a nearby towel.

Wrapping the soft terrycloth around herself, she strode to the mirror and wiped the steam with the side of her palm, clearing a ribbon of space. Dark circles shadowed her eyes. Her mascara had run when she'd cried and again when she'd dunked her head under water, leaving black streaks to stain her cheeks.

She tilted her head and leaned in, intrigued by the two crimson dots marring the pale flesh of her throat. She ran a fingertip over the marks. There was no pain but another flash of arousal pulsed in her cunt at the grazing touch.

"Not again," she murmured, dropping her hand.

She walked into her bedroom and threw open a window. While she'd bathed, it had begun to snow and the flakes rushing in on a gust of wind were icy against her flushed skin. Outside the snow was so thick it seemed solid, blurring the shapes of the city.

She inhaled deeply, grateful for the chill breeze cooling her overheated body. She needed to get out of New York, to put as much distance as she could between herself and Tristan.

But what if all the distance in the world won't be enough?

She shuddered, refusing to pursue that line of thought. A new start in the Florida Keys was just what she needed. After the fool she'd made of herself tonight, she was sure Tristan wouldn't pursue her. And even if he tried, her father would never tell him where she was.

Unless he used his IOU.

No. She couldn't think that way. Far from New York, she'd be safe from the aching desire, protected from Tristan's fierce, knowing gaze, from his passionate, impossible-to-resist touch.

And that was exactly what she wanted, she told herself as she flicked off the bedside lamp. The first light of dawn was breaking over the city and the snow cast a diamond-like sheen over her small apartment.

So then why did a cold chill of disappointment inch down her spine?

Chapter Five

ೞ

If the previous night had been one of the strangest in Tristan's entire existence, tonight was rapidly turning into one of the worst. He'd spent a good portion of the flight listening to Marie regale him with stories about the rumors flying around New York regarding his barely dressed state and his suicidal date.

"Hang on a second. The evening edition of the *Post* just arrived." There was a long pause during which Tristan rubbed the bridge of his nose and tried to keep a pounding migraine at bay.

He stared out the tinted windows of the limo his brother had thoughtfully sent to pick him up. It was smaller and more modern than his model, a sleek metallic silver rather than the black he favored. Still, the bar was well stocked with everything from little bottles of vodka to a small, ice-cold vial of O positive. He'd downed it immediately, the coppery taste doing little to take the edge off his hunger.

After tasting Lara's blood, he wasn't sure anything else would ever satisfy him. The strikingly vivid memory of the terror blazing in her eyes was so unexpected and painful that he gritted his teeth and dug his fingernails into his palm.

"Oh boss, you're not going to like this."

Tristan groaned. The limo turned left into a long driveway and came to a stop in front of a set of iron gates, which swung open at the car's approach. Two massive gargoyles watched the limo glide through from either side of the gate, their massive wings, claws and beaks all poised to strike.

Knowing Hayden, the gargoyles weren't just for show.

"Just tell me already and get it over with."

"Maybe I should show you instead. Check your phone."

He watched the status indicator on his cell flash red then green as a grainy image slowly took shape until it filled the small screen. "You have got to be kidding me."

"I'm afraid not," Marie said ruefully. "And the write-up is even worse."

Tristan gawked at a black and white picture of himself flattened against his limo. It must have been taken just after the truck had sped by, missing him by a mere inch. A black privacy strip covered his crotch, so small that it barely hid his dick. The dark curls peeking from beneath the gaping zipper had been left exposed.

And that wasn't even the worst part.

His *fangs* were showing.

It wasn't until that exact moment that Tristan finally understood why people either loved or hated candid shots. He knew without a doubt he fell into the latter category.

Though the image had been printed in black and white, the lack of color didn't hide the twisted agony clearly written on Tristan's face. His eyes were wide as he stared straight into the camera. In truth, he'd been frantically trying to spot Lara, afraid that by the time he saw her, she'd be no more than a stain on the dark pavement.

Above the grainy photograph, thick black letters proclaimed, *Saint Exposes Himself, Angel Runs Away in Horror.*

"How could the write-up be worse than the headline?" he asked, glad he could no longer see the photo as he held the phone to his ear.

"Trust me. Whoever wrote this didn't pull any punches. He comes close to accusing you of stalking but never quite comes right out to say it."

Tristan frowned. "And who exactly am I supposed to have been stalking?"

"Lara Montgomery. Apparently someone saw you with her at Bitter Sweet the other night." Marie's tone turned playful. "You didn't tell me you brought a date to your meeting with Richard."

"She wasn't there as my date." He was going to say more but he clamped his mouth firmly shut. He'd gotten the distinct impression that Lara didn't want her father knowing where they'd met and there could only be one reason for that. Aside from Richard and now Tristan, it had dawned on him that it was likely no one else knew about her part-time job.

"Fine. Keep your secrets. But I need you back in town to do damage control."

"Money does the best damage control, Marie. You know that as well as I do."

"Perhaps. But I worked too hard on your reputation to have you besmirch it by bolting out in front of paparazzi with your pants around your ankles."

"My pants weren't—" He took a deep breath, willing his frustration to ebb. Marie's sense of humor usually suited him. Aside from his brothers, she was probably the only person in the world who could make a smart-mouthed remark at his expense and get away with it.

Tonight though, there was only one woman's mouth he wanted and she, like Marie, was still in New York. Probably getting the brunt of the gossipmongering.

He grimaced, wishing he could have spared her the embarrassment. If he'd known, he might even have swept her away on his jet, brought her to Florida before the story broke. He could have kept her here with him until the furor died down.

"By the way," Marie said. "Whatever happened to the rumor that vampires can't have their pictures taken?"

Tristan sighed. "Wouldn't that have been nice? There are many myths I wish were true. Like that mirror thing, for example. I'd give anything not to know when I'm having a bad hair day."

"Well, there is that. But if not for mirrors, how would you ever know if your zipper was down?"

Tristan snapped the cell phone shut, Marie's delighted giggles still ringing in his ear.

The woman's PR services may have been the best use of a silent IOU he'd ever thought up, but on some nights, he wished he'd never run across her family.

The limo wound its way up a long, stone-inlaid path. On either side, palm trees swung gently in the breeze. Hayden's mansion came into view slowly, as if rising out of the ocean itself.

Although this was Tristan's first visit to his brother's new home, Hayden had eagerly regaled him with stories of his architectural masterpiece when he'd had the place built. So Tristan shouldn't have been surprised when the structure came into view, but he still found himself gaping as the car came to a stop.

For a mansion, Hayden's wasn't very big. Boasting only two floors and a loft, the house was among the less imposing in the region. But Hayden had never been a man who cared much about size…except perhaps his own.

From the ground up, the Colonial-style architecture had been designed to be built entirely out of glass. Thin metal beams placed at odd angles held the panes together at seemingly random intervals. Every light in the house was on and Tristan could clearly make out interior glass walls, sleek metallic-themed furniture and a glass staircase leading to the second floor. He could even see the ocean behind the mansion as it billowed and churned, the silver moon casting a sparkling sheen over the dark, writhing mass.

All of which told him that his brother hadn't changed a bit.

Tristan didn't wait for the driver to open his door. He climbed out of the car and dashed up the small path then banged on the front door, feeling foolish. A man in a dark suit was already heading his way. No doubt having no impediments to his line of sight gave him plenty of warning that company had arrived.

"Mr. Chance. The master is expecting you." The man bowed low, a polite smile on his weather-worn brown skin.

Tristan returned the smile, trying not to roll his eyes. A butler too. Hayden didn't do anything in half measures.

"If you'll please wait in the living room, I'll inform the master you've arrived."

"He's here?" Tristan looked around, his gaze sweeping the entire length of the first floor. He hadn't seen anyone but the butler when the car pulled up.

The man inclined his head. "Of course. As I said, he's been expecting you."

With another sweeping bow, the butler turned on his heel and marched out of the room. Tristan followed him. He'd never been very good at taking orders, even well-intentioned, polite ones.

The butler must have known Tristan was right on his heels but he didn't slow or turn around. He walked into what Tristan guessed must have been a study. Low bookshelves lined the transparent room dividers and a glass fireplace sat cheerily in a corner. At least a dozen sketchbooks lay scattered around the room, half-finished designs sketched hastily on the top page of each.

The man stopped in front of a wooden panel laid into the floor, bent down and rapped on it three times.

Tristan shuffled from foot to foot, half expecting to be asked for a password.

The panel lifted, opening directly onto a set of stairs leading underground. Hayden bounded up the last few steps to the surface, a boyish grin on his handsome features. "Well,

well. If it isn't my super-important brother dropping in for a visit."

Despite his annoyance with Hayden's extravagance, Tristan clasped him in a warm embrace. "Tell me, little brother, why does a vampire live in a glass house?"

Hayden laughed. "Is that a trick question? Or can you think of a better way to ensure no one finds out what I really am?"

Tristan shook his head, having to concede Hayden had a point. He stepped back to look at his brother. Though only four years younger than Tristan, Hayden had always been the easygoing, carefree one of the bunch. He'd inherited their father's gold-speckled green eyes, but that's where the family resemblance between them ended.

All three Chance brothers had been sired with different women and Hayden had taken after his mother. Blond highlights flashed through his tousled brown hair. His sculpted cheekbones, sharp jaw and permanent stubble gave him the appearance of a male model, an image Hayden carefully groomed by wearing soft white shirts unbuttoned at the throat, revealing a sprinkling of dark chest hair.

A gold cross hung on a chain around his neck, debunking yet another vampire myth.

"Will there be anything else, sir?"

Hayden shook his head. "That's it for tonight, Simon. Why don't you head on home?"

"Yes, sir."

Hayden waited until the butler departed then turned to Tristan, the smile vanishing as his eyes flashed hot with excitement. "Is it true? Have you finally met her?"

Tristan turned away, unable to meet his brother's gaze, and focused on the churning froth dancing across the ocean's surface. "I'm not sure."

"Tell me about her."

Tristan took a deep breath. Just thinking about Lara swamped him with longing.

Reluctantly he told his brother everything, beginning with the first time he saw her and ending with the newspaper article. When he finished, he found himself slumped in an oversized lounger on top of a white velvet throw. Though it should have been tacky, Tristan found the soft warmth comforting instead.

"Why do you insist in denying what you know to be true?" Hayden asked after a long pause. "You've met her. You've touched her. You've seen the way she ran from you. She's yours, Tristan, whether you believe it or not."

Tristan wanted to argue but what could he say? The fact that he was even here spoke volumes. And besides, he knew Hayden was right. He'd known it from the moment he'd first laid eyes on Lara. He'd felt it when they touched. He'd even told her as much while he thrust his fingers in her pussy, eagerly needing to see her topple over the edge and give in to the ecstasy only he could bring her.

His fangs had begun to extend just thinking of Lara and he ran the tip of his tongue over one. "A long time ago, I thought I'd met my soul mate," he said softly. "I was wrong then."

Hayden stood by his side and placed a hand on his shoulder. "Just because you were wrong then doesn't mean you're wrong now."

Tristan took a deep breath, fighting back the painful memories that threatened to spill out from the walled-off part of his heart. "I really thought Jane was the one. I pushed her and I shouldn't have. I turned her and she couldn't take it."

"It was almost three hundred years ago and *we* turned her," Hayden corrected him. "You can't do it alone. And you can't take all the blame, no matter how much you might want to."

Tristan leaned his head back and closed his eyes, remembering an evening much like this one. That night, with his brothers by his side, he'd brought his young wife of two months into his new life. He thought he was offering her eternal bliss, eternal love.

He should have known from the moment she rejected the joining ceremony that she wasn't cut out to be a creature of the night. She'd struggled the entire time Tristan and his brothers had tried to bring her pleasure, to take her into that wild frenzy of desire that would make turning her possible.

In the end she'd given in, but only, he now believed, because she gave up the fight. She lasted two days as a vampire before she walked outside at dawn while Tristan slept. He awoke to a pile of ashes in his front yard and knew without a doubt that his shattered heart lay in those ashes with her.

"I can't turn Lara," he said firmly. "I won't."

"You don't have to. But you do have to put a stop to this curse if you want to keep her." Hayden shot Tristan a sidelong glance. "Vampires can take human companions. We can love mortal women, even if it's for a short while."

"You don't really believe in that 'it's better to have loved and lost than never to have loved at all' bullshit, do you?" He hated the venom in his voice but he couldn't help it. Would a lifetime with Lara ever be enough to quench the burning thirst surging through his soul? Simply touching her made his blood burn hot and his cock stiffen. He'd never felt that kind of attraction to anyone in his entire existence. Not even to his wife.

That thought should have made him feel guilty but it didn't. He felt nothing but remorse at what he'd done to her, but no more.

He looked up to see Hayden's jaw clenched tight, his hands balled into fists by his sides. "Don't talk to me about loss," he rasped. "I've followed my true mate through three of her mortal lifetimes, always knowing I couldn't keep her, always unable to stop the inevitable from happening, no matter how much I wanted to." He stalked to the window then turned, jabbing a finger in Tristan's direction. "Don't you talk to me about loss!"

Tristan inclined his head and sucked in an anguished breath. "I'm sorry. I didn't mean—"

"Of course you did. You've never believed me before. Every time I came to you drowning in sorrow, every time I needed you to believe me, you turned me away."

"I just didn't think—"

"No. You didn't." Hayden sighed, the anger dissipating into thin air as quickly as it had manifested. "But now you do."

"The curse is real." It felt odd saying that, but in a positive way. As though a heavy weight he'd carried around with him for much too long had finally been lifted off his chest.

"Let me show you something."

Tristan watched as Hayden disappeared beneath the wooden panel. This time he didn't feel the need to follow.

A few minutes later his brother returned, holding a leather-bound book. "This is all the information I've managed to collect. It's not much, but it's all I have."

Tristan flipped the front cover open, quickly realizing it wasn't a book at all, but a journal. The yellowing paper was brittle and slightly stained. Hayden had filled many of the pages with his messy oversized script. Maps and sketches of various seemingly unrelated objects had been hastily drawn, showing items ranging from a chalice to a log cabin.

He turned the pages, scanning the contents, unsure what he should be looking for. Then his gaze fell on a family tree and he followed the branches with his index finger. "Who was Calvin Chance?"

"The man who got us into this mess six hundred years ago."

"He cursed our family?"

Hayden shook his head. "Indirectly maybe. From what I've been able to discover, the curse was actually cast by a witch who lived a few houses down from him." He tapped the opposite side of the page. "Katherine Smith."

"What did he do to anger her? And more importantly, why take it out on his entire bloodline?"

Hayden shrugged. "That I don't know. But it gets worse."

Tristan's stomach twisted sharply. "How could it get worse?"

"That's what I tried to tell you on the phone when you called last night but you wouldn't listen."

"I'm listening now."

Hayden's eyes flared with a dark intensity Tristan rarely saw in his upbeat brother's gaze. "If you don't find a way to put a stop to the curse permanently in seven..." He hesitated, flicking the tip of his tongue over his lips. "Wait, you first saw Lara on Saturday night?"

Tristan nodded, not trusting himself to speak.

"In four days, Lara is going to die."

Chapter Six

ം

Tristan's laugh bounced off the glass enclosures, echoing like the dying wail of a banshee through the room. "Your jokes used to be much funnier, little brother."

Hayden met his gaze full on without flinching. No hint of a smile tugged at his lips. "I wish it were a joke. If it were, we could have a good laugh about the way I had to suffer through losing my life mate three times in three centuries. I'm *not* laughing."

Tristan's vision clouded. He gripped the chair's armrests tightly as he waited for the wave of nausea to pass. This wasn't happening to him again.

God, not again.

"Why?" His strangled whisper sounded hollow, defeated. "How?"

"A million different ways or none at all. Freak accidents. A natural disaster. I don't know. All I know is that the clock starts ticking the first time you see her." Hayden's voice shook. He cleared his throat but it was too late. Tristan's heart clenched at the thought of his brother grieving the loss of his mate repeatedly, alone simply because Tristan had been too foolish and hardheaded to believe him.

"As for why," Hayden continued, "if I knew that, I'd have a lot more to show for my efforts." He pointed to the journal Tristan still clutched in his hands.

Tristan's head pounded, an aching, throbbing pain that started behind his eyes and swept to the base of his neck. Something gripped his heart—a feeling he couldn't recognize at first, though he should have. He'd caused it enough times.

Fear.

"I have to stop it." He rose from the chair, took a step toward the door and felt his knees give way.

Hayden was at his side in a flash of movement, his hand reaching out to steady him. The amber specks in his green eyes glowed with an intensity Tristan had never seen before.

"When was the last time you fed?"

Tristan pulled out of his brother's grip and waved him away, silently relieved to find he could stand on his own. "I snacked in the limo. A vial of that stuff you keep took the edge off. Before that…last night." His mouth went dry. Lust flashed through his veins, instantly tensing his muscles, stiffening his cock. "From Lara."

"You can't do that again."

Tristan lifted a shoulder in a half shrug. "You're right. She's in New York while I'm stuck here, too far away to protect her."

"The only person you need to protect her from right now is you. She's vulnerable to you. The curse will have made sure of it. Staying away is the best thing you can do for her."

"Like hell." He strode to the door while yanking his cell phone from his jacket. "I'm going to have the jet prepared for take off. I have to warn Lara. I have to—"

The world went black.

* * * * *

The coppery scent of blood beckoned, summoning Tristan from a dark, dreamless sleep. He blinked his eyes open, surprised to find himself looking up at Hayden. His brother held an uncapped blood vial before his nose.

"Drink."

Hayden tipped the vial, the crimson liquid spilling between Tristan's lips, drenching his mouth with its metallic flavor. He swallowed greedily, recognizing the flavor as the same one he'd tasted earlier in the limo. The same person? A donor?

Thoughts jumbled through his mind in a haze. Lara. Hayden. The curse. Strength flooded his veins, poured through his body in a fevered rush as the elixir that would sustain him cascaded down his throat.

When the last drop had poured out of the small container, Tristan reached out instinctively, sucking at the small opening.

"That's the last one. If you want more, we'll have to go out."

A growl broke free from Tristan's chest. He lunged to his feet, grabbed his brother by the shirt collar and shoved him backward until he slammed into the glass wall. Hayden didn't flinch but a thin line split the wall as the glass cracked from the force of the impact.

Hayden sighed. *Are you done? Or would breaking my house apart make you feel better?*

The telepathic link flared between them, the blood tie humming along his skin, as much a part of him as his hunger.

Tristan pushed back from the wall, his lips peeled back from his teeth in frustration, his fangs fully extended. "I need to put an end to this curse and I need to do it *now*."

"I haven't found a way to do that in three centuries." Hayden's tone wasn't mocking but that didn't help Tristan's mood.

He paced the length of the floor, running his hand through his unbound hair. "There are two of us now, little brother. We'll find a way to do this."

"Fine. But unless you want to pass out again in an hour, you need to feed."

Tristan released a deep breath on a whoosh of air. He didn't want to feed. Sure, he wanted—needed—the sustenance blood gave him, but he knew the intimate connection he'd have to forge to get it. Drinking from Lara had been incredible, giving him a rush he'd never before experienced.

A shiver ran through him. Hunger burned through his veins, leaving a hot, aching need in its wake. His cock pulsed as he conjured up a mental image of Lara, her wide, dark eyes glazed with lust instead of terror, her parted lips glistening wetly, inviting him to capture her taste in his mouth.

The connection between them had been unmistakable. It lit a blazing fire in his veins, made his entire being throb with barely contained desire.

How could he share that kind of intimacy with another woman after being with Lara? After learning—*knowing*—she was his soul mate?

After he was turned, Tristan had quickly come to realize that there was only one way to ensure he fed properly without harming his victim. A woman's pain and pleasure receptors were intricately linked and the moment of orgasm provided the perfect opportunity to fulfill both their deepest desires.

When they'd lived together, Tristan, Hayden and Alexander often fed simultaneously, at times seeking out two, three victims a night. They'd learned early on that sharing could be more satisfying than dining alone.

In less than a day, all that had changed. Tristan didn't want to find a woman with whom to spend the night. He wanted Lara in his arms, in his bed. He needed his cock buried deep in her hot, moist core, his fangs embedded in her silky flesh, her warm blood spilling down his throat.

Hayden placed a hand on his shoulder and gave him a sympathetic half smile. "I know." He didn't have to say anything more. The blood link was strong enough to project Tristan's emotions and besides, his feelings were probably written all over his face. "But you need this."

"What I need is to find a way to end this fucking curse." He practically spat the words out between his teeth.

Hayden frowned. "If I can lead you to someone who can provide a link to Katherine Smith, then will you feed?"

"Someone else knows of the witch? Who?"

"Her name is Illiana. She's a descendant of Katherine's and lives here in town along with her brother."

Excitement coiled low in Tristan's stomach. Finally some sort of lead he could pursue, someone he could question. He slid the journal in the front pocket of his jacket. "Let's go."

Hayden grimaced. "I should probably tell you she doesn't know anything about the curse."

Tristan shrugged. "Maybe you're just not asking the right questions."

Twenty minutes later they strolled along the dark boardwalk bordering the beach. Hayden lived on a small inlet, an island community that boasted only one tourist resort. In December, tourist season in the Florida Keys died down and it showed. They passed only a handful of people as they walked from Hayden's mansion into town.

To their right, there was nothing but sand and beach. To their left, there was more sand, palm trees and a string of impressive Victorian homes, many much grander than Hayden's. Most of the owners had hung Christmas lights around their windows and decorated the palm trees facing the ocean in the spirit of the season, despite the heat that made the holiday feel less than festive.

Tristan yearned for New York, for the white Christmas the weather forecasters had promised. It was only four days away, leaving plenty of time for the city to be blanketed in pure snow.

Four days. Lara would die on Christmas day.

He shook his head to dislodge that train of thought. Most of all, Tristan yearned for Lara. The few ounces of blood he'd ingested couldn't come close to the rapture that had enveloped him when he'd tasted hers. His entire body felt on edge, taut and ready to feed, yet his mind couldn't accept the knowledge that he had to be intimate with another woman to make that happen.

To assuage some of the frantic need pulsing through his veins, Tristan asked Hayden to tell him about his life mate. He listened intently as Hayden described first meeting her when he was still human. Only twenty-one at the time, he'd chalked up his passion for the young Isabelle as mere infatuation. He thought his obsession had more to do with the fact that she ran from him each time they made love than anything else. Accustomed to having women eager to obey his every whim, Hayden had enjoyed the challenge she'd presented. When she died in a tragic fire a week later, he'd mourned her but moved on.

When he ran across her again half a century later, he fell madly in love. She wasn't his Isabelle anymore, but Lydia, a blonde-haired, blue-eyed temptress working as a whore at a seaside tavern in Scotland. Still, something in his soul recognized her and his body had cried out for her. She filled every need, every burning desire. She even accepted his hunger, his ache for the precious blood pouring through her veins. Exactly five days from their first meeting, in her frenzy to get away from him, she leapt over the balcony railing. Her room had been on the third floor. By the time Hayden's orgasmic glow wore off long enough to realize she was gone and dive down after her, it was too late. Her neck had snapped on impact.

Hayden spoke of everything as though reading from a history book, with no inflection in his voice. Still, Tristan could feel the sorrow drenching his brother's soul. When he fell silent before reaching the third story, Tristan was grateful. He knew neither of them could stomach any more tales of loss.

"Where are we going?" Tristan asked at last. They'd been walking for almost thirty minutes. If he'd fed, they'd have used their supernatural speed to cut traveling time but as it were, he'd only be able to summon the strength for a lightning-fast flick of his wrist.

"To see a work of art."

Tristan waited but Hayden didn't elaborate. A soft breeze ruffled the palm leaves and scattered the sweet scent of a night-blooming flower around them. "And we couldn't take a car?"

Hayden shrugged. "I gave the driver the night off too. Besides, this isn't New York. We're not likely to get mugged in a dark alley."

For a moment, Tristan didn't recognize the laugh echoing down the boardwalk as his own. It sounded foreign and unexpected, though not unwelcome.

A few minutes later Hayden led them down a narrow alleyway onto a street filled with row after row of nondescript townhouses. Gone were the ornate mansions and the iron gates. Yet whatever this neighborhood lacked in adornment, it more than made up for in charm.

"We're here," Hayden announced, stopping in front of a house like all the others. The yard was neatly manicured with a trim lawn and delicate purple flowers planted along the edges of a narrow path leading to the door.

Unlike the other townhouses though, parked cars flooded this one's driveway as well as both sides of the street. On the porch, half a dozen people leaned against a whitewashed railing. The sounds of their laughter and the scent of tobacco floated over the yard.

"Shit," Hayden said. "I forgot about the showing. I didn't think anyone would be here tonight."

Tristan raised an eyebrow. The mortal scents of lust and too much cologne flooded his senses. He could hear blood rushing through burning veins, pumping wildly as couples pressed against each other, sharing drunken kisses on the front porch.

"The what?"

"Illiana is an artist. She's having her first public showing tonight." He blew out a deep breath then inclined his head in the direction of the house. "Come on. I'm guessing you won't let a few dozen people stand in your way."

Tristan shook his head, the motion sending another jolt of nausea into his stomach. He needed to feed deeply and soon. "Lead on."

They followed a narrow concrete path to the front door then stepped over the threshold into a large living room. The furniture didn't match the modest look of the townhouse. Between the Asian rugs, velvet-draped couches, elegantly curtained windows, gold-gilded mirrors and the cathedral ceiling, it felt as though he'd just stepped into a private wing of a royal castle. Artwork lined the walls, mounted in thick frames decorated with sparkling beads and glass mosaics. The colors contrasted sharply with the black and white effects of Illiana's art.

"Charcoal?"

"Yes. She's quite good."

Tristan stepped closer to one of the images and was forced to agree. The sketch depicted a woman lying on an old-fashioned fainting couch, a man kneeling at her side. One arm was draped over her forehead while the other hung limply at her side. The man's mouth was clamped around her wrist. In addition to the charcoal, she'd used a few drops of red around the man's lips to bring a splash of color to the canvas.

"Hayden? I didn't expect to see you tonight."

Tristan turned around in time to see a woman dressed in a tight, beaded red dress head for his brother, arms outstretched. Her mass of blonde hair had been piled on top of her head in an elaborate updo and her crimson lips revealed perfect white teeth. She gave Tristan a leisurely once-over. "And who might this be?"

"Illiana, this is my brother Tristan. He's come all the way from New York so let's make him feel welcome, okay?"

"I've been told I'm good at that." Illiana laughed, a self-indulgent sound that grated on Tristan's nerves and made him longingly think of Lara's husky voice, of the way it slid down his skin and tightened his balls, deepening his craving. God, how he wanted her. As soon as this was over, he'd find her and fuck her for days, delighting in her body in every way possible.

A grin still plastered on Illiana's too-red lips, she leaned in and gazed into Tristan's eyes. "My…you look hungry. We can't have that." She tsked twice, her tongue smacking against her teeth. Tristan fought the urge to clench his fists.

You expect me to drink from her? he asked his brother, his eyes never leaving the woman.

I expect you to feed, yes. Leave the sex up to me if you'd like. I'll be more than happy to indulge for both of us. As though to demonstrate, he ran his palm over the woman's hip then slid his hand behind her to cup her ass. She giggled and pretended to swat Hayden's hand away.

I take it you two are well acquainted.

Hayden shrugged. *At first it was all about the curse. Now…well, I guess you can say we meet each other's needs.*

Tristan didn't doubt it. Judging by the heat rising from her body and the flush suffusing her cheeks, he'd say she was very familiar with Hayden. With what he was—what they both were.

She's your donor. It wasn't a question. He'd have recognized her taste as soon as he drank anyway and Hayden knew it too.

She's willing, if that's what you're wondering.

Tristan stifled a groan. In three hundred years, he'd never taken a donor. Hayden, on the other hand, had never had a problem with the concept. A walking, talking, willing blood bank. What could be better?

Sure, they sounded good in theory, but for Tristan, they were too much trouble. Donors had to be kept happy and he didn't relish the idea of being intimately tied to a woman who could reveal his deepest secret in a jealous fit. Besides, while he had no problem delivering orgasms on demand, most donors wanted payment for their services too.

He glanced over Illiana's shoulder at the ornately decorated house, guessing she probably wouldn't have been able to afford half the luxurious items she owned if not for his brother.

"Come with me." Illiana reached for Tristan's hand and pulled him after her as she turned and led the way through a cluster of people gathered around an elaborate sketch. "Stay, drink, enjoy yourselves," she called out to the crowd. "I have some personal business to attend to but I'll be back soon."

A couple of catcalls accompanied them as they climbed a set of stairs leading to the second floor. Otherwise no one seemed to notice or care that their hostess was leaving.

"My studio is up here." She pointed to a long railing draped with a flowing velvet curtain that took up the entire length of one wall. "I had it converted into a loft."

Sounds expensive.

Hayden narrowed his eyes and shook his head in silent admonishment. *She gives me what I need.*

With every step he climbed, Tristan's hunger grew. He felt a shift in atmosphere, a sudden heat that slid over his skin. He turned in mid-step, his gaze sweeping over the crowd. A flash of midnight black caught his eye. His breath caught in his throat. He blinked hard but found himself staring at a dark ebony sculpture.

"What is it?" Hayden asked, his brows drawn together in concern.

Tristan shook his head. "Nothing."

Need and desire blended together to form an agony-inducing swirl of ravenous craving. His fangs elongated and he flashed them briefly at Illiana. She parted her lips, her breathing quickening as she glanced from Tristan to Hayden then back again. "Let me show you my favorite painting."

At the top of the stairs they stopped in front of a set of double doors. Illiana fished a key from her cleavage, drawing Tristan's gaze to her tits. He remembered Lara's breasts, so perky and perfect, her nipples tightly beaded for him.

Illiana unlocked the door quickly, ushered them inside then closed it behind her.

She walked through the deep shadows to a corner of the room and turned on a floor lamp. Soft, yellow light infused the studio with a surreal glow.

The loft was half the size of the living room but just as richly decorated. Charcoal sketches lay scattered across every surface. A large bed took up the center of the room while a long, old-fashioned cream-colored fainting couch sat in front of the curtains. He recognized it as the one from Illiana's sketch.

The sounds of idle chitchat and laughter drifted up from the living room. The curtains hadn't been drawn tightly enough and the gap between them allowed Tristan to look out over the gathered crowd.

Once again his skin buzzed with sensual awareness. A deep, primal yearning settled low in his groin, making him shudder.

Illiana came up behind him and wrapped her arms around his waist. "Let's see if we can satisfy those carnal needs of yours, hmm?" She nipped at his earlobe.

Tristan shrugged out of her grasp and turned around to face her. Hayden pressed against her back, lowered his head and nipped playfully at the woman's throat. He hadn't broken the skin but Illiana shuddered as the spicy musk of her arousal seeped from between her legs and teased Tristan's nostrils.

His cock twitched, hardening against his pants despite himself. His fangs dug into his lower lip, eager to taste her, needing to feed.

He reached out and palmed her breasts through the beaded dress. She arched her back, pressing her taut nipples against his hands. "Oh yes, yes, yes," she murmured, each word a desperate plea for more.

The sound of a zipper being lowered resonated through the room, much too loudly to Tristan's sensitive ears. Illiana leaned forward, letting the straps of her dress fall over her shoulders.

Her tits bounced freely, two large mounds that spilled over Tristan's hands. He yearned for Lara's breasts, for her moans, as he squeezed the tight nipples between thumb and forefinger.

Illiana purred, a low, throaty sound infused with the promise of sinful pleasure. The hoarse moan turned into a cry as he twisted her nipples, reveling in the way her face contorted with pain while she panted, thrusting her chest out for more.

"Hurt me," she pleaded. "Take me."

God, but this is much too easy.

And now you see why donors are a good thing, his brother countered.

They moved around Illiana as though engaged in a sensual dance. Centuries of sharing a woman allowed them to pleasure the female body until they drove her over the edge, into a world of bliss she wouldn't otherwise experience.

Hayden removed Illiana's dress then her panties. She stepped out of her high-heeled sandals, standing naked before them. He shifted to kneel in front of her and parted her thighs open with his hands.

Tristan shifted to stand behind her. Sweat beaded at her temples and ran down the back of her neck. A blue vein throbbed just beneath her skin. Tristan licked his lips, knowing she'd be his in only a few more moments.

Patience, Hayden urged.

Tristan didn't need to be reminded. He'd heard the horrendous screams ripped from a woman's throat if he drank from her before she'd hit that pinnacle of climax. He had no desire to ever hear them again.

She bent her knees as Hayden clamped his mouth tightly on her pussy. Her entire body shuddered as she leaned forward slightly, thrusting out her ass.

Tristan ran his palms over the globes of her cheeks, parting them to peer at the puckered hole of her anus, which gaped open slightly under his scrutiny. He traced the rosebud with a fingertip. "You like that, do you?"

She whimpered in response, bending even farther from the waist. He slipped his finger inside, feeling her muscles clench around him, welcoming him in her tight, hot channel.

God, he wanted to do this to Lara—this and so much more. He wanted her bent over, ripe and yearning for him. His finger slid in past the knuckle. Illiana gasped, her muscles rigid beneath his hand.

He reached around her waist and pulled her upright, settling his fangs at the base of her neck and shoulder, his fingertip making slow, sensual circles inside her anus.

Illiana moved in rhythm to his thrusts and Hayden's tongue, her gasps of pleasure turning into high-pitched moans. Tristan could hear the frantic beat of her heart as it hammered against her ribs.

When she came, it was with a scream. Tristan didn't care. He sank his fangs into her flesh, his body shuddering with satisfaction as the coppery taste of her blood poured through his mouth.

She thrashed beneath him while Hayden embedded his fangs in her thigh. Hayden's blood lust took over, joining with Tristan's through their link and driving them both forward— sucking, drinking, swallowing her essence with thick, desperate gulps.

She cried out again, her orgasm clenching her inner muscles tighter around his finger. When Tristan released her, she pitched forward, losing her balance. With one hand, she steadied herself by grasping Hayden's shoulders. With the other, she yanked the curtains, pulling them and the rod down to clatter on the floor.

An assembled gasp echoed from the living room. Dozens of pairs of eyes stared up at them, some in wide-eyed wonder, others in appreciation.

Tristan only cared about one pair of eyes. The dark, luminous pair that only a night ago had been filled with terror.

Now, Lara's gaze swam with shock, recognition and the unmistakable glaze of betrayal.

Chapter Seven

ဢ

Lara's pulse thrummed a frenzied beat, her heart hammering so hard it made it almost impossible to breathe. Instinctively, her hand shot out for support and clamped around a masculine arm.

"Wow. When I said I wanted to take you out for dinner and a show, this wasn't exactly what I had in mind."

She glanced at the man standing beside her as though seeing him for the first time. Slight of build with wavy brown hair that fell into his eyes and black-rimmed glasses, he had a genuine smile. Best yet, there was nothing the least bit dangerous about him. Her father would approve.

He worked in the human resources department of the Montgomery Suites Resort, and when he'd asked her out, she'd only hesitated for a moment, grateful for anything that might take her mind off Tristan.

Her brows furrowed. What was his name? *Michael? Mitch?*

"Miguel." She pulled her hand back. Tears stung her eyes and she ground her teeth together, determined not to look up again.

Her resolve lasted for about two seconds. Had it really been Tristan? Or had she merely conjured his image out of her fevered fantasies?

Since she'd last seen him a night ago, she'd been able to think of nothing else. Her flight to Florida was a distant, hazy memory. She remembered spending it curled up in her seat under an airline blanket, her palm pressed firmly against her cunt.

She glanced at the railing but he was gone. A tall, blondish man helped the woman into her dress. Neither one seemed to care they had an audience.

"I'm sorry you had to see that," Miguel said. "Maybe we should leave."

"Leave?" She knew she sounded like a fool but she couldn't concentrate. Tristan was here, in this room. She could feel it in the way her jittery nerves zipped across her skin, the way her pussy clenched in anticipation.

Miguel slid his hand into hers. It felt clammy and too warm against her palm. He turned toward the door and she spun around to follow but came to an abrupt stop when she slammed into a rock-solid chest.

The man was at least five inches taller and his broad shoulders blocked out the rest of the room. Her breath skidded to a stop. She didn't even have to look at his face to recognize him. "Tristan."

His green eyes blazed into hers. "You're coming with me."

"I'm not going anywhere." She tried to lace her voice with exasperation but her entire body hummed at the sound of his words. Since running away the night before, she'd wanted nothing more but to be in his arms.

At least until she'd seen him with another woman. She hadn't been able to make out exactly what he'd been doing to her but by her flushed cheeks and unabashed screams, she doubted he'd been whispering poetry.

Anger flickered in his gaze and his features grew hard, his lips pressing into a thin line. She fought the urge to take a step back.

"What's this all about?" Miguel asked. "I'm sure we can–"

She didn't know whether Miguel ever finished his sentence. Tristan leapt toward her with a speed that should have been impossible. She barely saw him as he slid one arm around her waist, another around her knees, and pressed her against his chest.

"Wait— Stop— You can't—" The words tumbled out of her mouth then disappeared on a rush of air.

They sped through the crowd with breathtaking swiftness. She saw people stumbling to get out of the way. Those who weren't quick enough landed on the floor as the force of Tristan's rapid stride slammed into them.

Miguel shouted something in their wake but by then they were outside, blazing through the shadows. Warm night air slid against her skin as Tristan streaked down a back alley then turned left—or was it right?—on to the boardwalk. Ocean waves crashed against the shore, the sound merging with the gust of wind roaring in her ears.

The trip lasted no more than a minute but when Tristan finally stopped, they were on a deserted strip of the beach, much farther away than they should have been.

"God." Lara exhaled as the breath left her lungs. She tightened her hold around Tristan's neck, dizziness threatening to overwhelm her.

Her heart pounded against his chest, hammering a mile a minute, yet Tristan didn't even seem winded. In a flash, he'd taken them miles from where they'd been.

She could no longer see any landmark she recognized, she thought warily as she opened her eyes and glanced over his shoulder. In the distance, the blue and red neon sign of Montgomery Suites flickered against the inky black sky. It was as though he'd brought her to their own peaceful, private oasis in the middle of a busy, demanding world.

"Why aren't you in New York?" she managed to whisper.

In response, his mouth slammed down on hers hard. She moaned and clenched her hands into fists, intending to push him away. Every warning her father and brother had given her slithered through her mind. A million protests entered her brain but she couldn't voice them. His tongue pressed against her lips, demanding entry.

He tasted like copper and cinnamon gum, and he smelled like arousal.

Another woman's arousal.

His muscles stiffened and he stopped his assault on her mouth. Instead he licked her lower lip, the move infinitely tender, unexpectedly gentle.

Arrogance she expected. The need for control she could withstand. Tenderness however, was entirely foreign.

Her defenses crumbled under his sensual kiss.

She sighed and opened to him. His tongue slid inside her mouth, silky and moist. He circled hers slowly, moving with care, as though suddenly afraid to hurt her.

Lara's hands brushed over his shoulders, feeling the corded length of his muscles bunch beneath her touch. He still wore his elegant suit, even here, despite the warm heat lingering in the night air.

The soft fabric of his jacket molded to his broad shoulders and she trailed her palms around the front of his chest, eager to feel more of him. She thrust her fingers beneath the silk lining, caressing his chest as he tore down all her well-built resistance with sweep after sweep of his tongue against hers.

Her pussy pulsed in response to the needy, yearning ache that started low in her stomach and traveled lower still. Cream dampened the crotch of her panties. She tried to rub her thighs together, to press against the demanding need, but Tristan still held her in his arms and squirming only shoved her firmly against his chest.

Why is he here? What was he doing with that woman?

More importantly, what was he doing *to* her?

Tristan tore his mouth away, emotions flickering over his face. She thought she saw doubt and uncertainly flash in his eyes but they didn't linger, and soon she was staring at the confident man she'd first met three days ago.

She swallowed hard. Had it only been three days? Her primal attraction to him, her eager lust, it couldn't all be explained away as infatuation with a man she'd only known for less than a week.

Could it?

"I wasn't there for Illiana." Tristan didn't release her. Instead, he nuzzled her throat, sending a delicious shiver down the curve of her spine.

"You don't owe me an explanation."

She meant it, though she wished she hadn't seen him with someone else. But how hypocritical could she be? Hadn't she done the same thing with Miguel? Well, all right, maybe not quite the same thing...but the intent had been there, and if given a chance, she might have followed through, just as he had.

Moonlight careened over his unbound hair, sparkling off his darkened gaze. His lips turned downward into a slight frown but he didn't try to clarify the situation. She didn't need a blow-by-blow account of what had happened up in that loft. She'd heard the woman's screams, she'd seen the man kneeling before her. And she'd seen Tristan bent over her naked form, his lips pressed to her neck in an intimate, powerfully suggestive act.

"I didn't want her." Releasing a deep sigh, he placed Lara on her feet then slipped his arm around her waist and pulled her to him. "I want you." His erection pressed against the soft silk of her shirt and into her stomach. Her knees nearly buckled at the feel of his thick cock.

She remembered the girth and length of it, the silky softness of his skin, the beaded moisture that had dripped from the tip.

Cupping his hard shaft in her hand, she ran her palm over the bulge tenting his pants. "You only want me because you couldn't have me," she retorted then held her breath. Until that moment, she hadn't considered the full implication of that thought. Had he pursued her across the country simply because she'd run from him? If she'd spent the night, would he have forgotten all about her the next morning?

Or did he want her only because he knew her father wouldn't allow it? Tristan was handsome, powerful and rich. How many women would gladly fall into his bed if he as much as looked in their direction?

She shuddered. She didn't want to think about anyone else in Tristan's bed or in his arms. She wiped away the mental image of him leaning over Illiana.

He ran his fingertips down her cheek and along her jaw. Lowering his mouth, he thrust his hips forward, his erection boldly demanding. "You don't believe that."

She licked her lips. "I'm not sure what to believe."

"Then give me an hour to prove it."

Before she could ask what he meant, he was on his knees, pulling the hem of her skirt up around her hips. She glanced around wildly but this part of the beach was empty with the exception of a few gulls and a crab that had washed ashore.

"We can't... Not here..."

Her protests fell on deaf ears, or perhaps she hadn't uttered them at all. Excitement pumped through her, sending a rushing stream of heat between her legs. Arousal mingled with the scent of the ocean, imbuing her musky aroma with a salty fragrance. Her nipples tightened in anticipation.

"You've got such a hot little pussy under all those clothes," Tristan murmured. He trailed his fingertip along the thin barrier of her cotton panties. She wished she'd worn something sexier, something that would guarantee he couldn't keep his hands off her.

Not that it looked as though he were having trouble with that particular task.

The crotch of her underwear was damp and it stuck to her labia as he pressed his fingers against her cunt, trailing a smooth line up and down her slit. Shivers of delight ran through her. She trembled and fought for control, but he had no intention of stopping.

Tristan pulled her panties to the side, the same way he'd done in the limo. Except now she was on her feet, standing on legs she wasn't sure could support her if he touched her again, if he thrust any part of his anatomy inside her.

He cupped her mound intimately, the heel of his palm pressing against her clit, his fingers seeking then finding her soaked entrance.

"You're so wet," he groaned. "Is this all for me?"

She bit down on her lower lip hard. She didn't want him to know how much he affected her but feared it was too late for that now. He already knew how her pussy reacted to him. What could she say that would be more revealing than that?

"I want to taste you." He looked up, his gaze earnest and perhaps a little uncertain, though she could have been imagining the latter. "Will you let me?"

A protest lodged in her throat. One word had the power to push him away, perhaps for good. She could deny him what they both wanted and she could go on with her life while trying to forget she'd ever run into Tristan Chance.

Yes.

He grinned and pulled her panties over her hips and down her thighs, baring her pussy. His mouth moved closer. Then, as though realizing she hadn't yet answered his question, he gazed up at her. "Will you let me?" he repeated. This time, the words were brazen, confident. He knew she wouldn't deny him.

"God help me," she murmured, tangling her fingers in his hair. "Yes."

He didn't hesitate. His tongue shot out, reaching her throbbing, pulsing clit a second before his mouth latched on to her cunt. She held on tightly to his thick mane while he licked her, the intimacy of the act making her cry out.

What if someone came by? There was no barrier between this section of the beach and any other, though they were close to the reefs and it was past midnight on a weeknight. The chances of someone stumbling upon them during a late-night stroll were slim but her nervous gaze still shifted along the length of the beach, analyzing every slinking shadow dotting the ground.

Tristan's lips burned with a tender heat that traveled into her cunt and spread through her body, turning her muscles to a trembling, unsteady mass.

"Tristan, please," she whimpered, barely recognizing her own voice.

She was so close, so very, very close. Her climax hovered just out of reach as he teased her slowly, mercilessly, his tongue lapping at her slit but never centering on the pulsing nub that demanded his undivided attention.

And still, she knew he had only to touch her clit and she'd shatter. "I need…"

His nose brushed against her mound, close, yet not close enough. Lust raged through her in a roaring torrent, demanding release. She yanked his hair and pulled him nearer still, craving the orgasm as she craved the air filling her lungs.

At the last moment, just when she thought she couldn't possibly take any more and she'd come from just another lick, he stopped. Something tore inside her and a cry wrenched free from her chest filled the air. The loss of the satisfaction he'd been promising clogged her throat with a disappointment so deep she thought it would engulf her.

She gasped, a strangled noise that sounded pathetic to her own ears. She reached down to touch herself, knowing that if she didn't come, she'd lose her mind.

He grabbed both her wrists and stood, drawing her arms up over her head and pinning them together. She struggled against him, rubbing her pussy against his thigh.

"Not yet, sweetheart," he whispered in her ear, the maddening sound of his voice making her tremble. "We need to talk first."

"T-talk?" she stuttered, uncomprehending. They didn't need to talk. They communicated just fine without words.

"I'm going to release your hands now, but only if you promise you'll be good. Let me be the only one to touch your pussy tonight. In return, I promise you'll have what you crave."

She bit her lower lip and ground her teeth together, glaring at him. If she didn't do as he asked, she'd have her orgasm. She knew just what her body needed. She could bring herself to climax in the span of three seconds since her entire being already hovered on the brink of ecstasy.

But if she did, she had a feeling he wouldn't touch her again and she couldn't bear that. "I won't come," she promised him, dragging in a deep breath meant to calm her pounding heart. "But only on one condition."

He chuckled, the warmth of his laughter grazing her skin. "What's that?"

"You fuck me first and *then* we'll talk. Because if you don't, so help me God, I'm not going to be held responsible for my actions."

"Mmm…you drive a hard bargain." He swept his tongue over her lips. When she opened her mouth, he dove in for a brief moment, but that was all it took for the taste of her juices to assault her senses and flood her with a new wave of arousal.

He released her hands and stepped back, a grin tugging at the corners of his mouth. For a moment, she feared he'd say no. Her heart beat a frenzied rhythm against her rib cage but calmed when she noticed the admiration mixing with the unmistakable lust on his features. He shrugged out of his jacket and laid it on the sand.

Giddy excitement built inside Lara, sending a jolt of electricity skidding down her skin. She'd won! She'd actually stood up to a man who loved being in control and she'd gotten what she wanted.

He hadn't even tried to argue or bully her into getting his way. And this was only the beginning. Soon, she'd have the release she craved and then she'd demand more and more and more. She'd make him pleasure her until the early hours of the morning, until the sun came up and she lay spent, unable to move from sheer exhaustion.

Her smile flared into a full-fledged grin. She watched, her fingers clenching and unclenching at her sides as he unbuckled his pants. Her cunt craved attention, begged for it with small throbbing spasms, but she'd promised him she wouldn't touch herself and she intended to keep that promise. Besides, she wouldn't have to wait much longer.

His belt came off with a snap of leather that made her knees buckle. She could almost feel the sting of the belt slapping against her ass. She squirmed and pressed her thighs together. A stream of liquid heat slid down her inner thigh.

Next, Tristan pulled down his zipper, so slowly she yearned to close the distance between them and do it for him in one smooth motion that would free his cock.

At long last, he slid his pants and boxers over his hips. He kicked off his shoes and peeled off his socks. A moment later, his shirt and tie followed. He heaped everything in a pile beside his jacket and stood naked, the silvery sheen of moonlight dancing over the planes of his chest and glinting off the drop of moisture gathered at the tip of his rod.

He cupped his shaft, pulling it away from his body, and stroked the thick length with quick, practiced movements.

Lara took a step forward. Now that she had him just where she wanted him, she was dismayed to find her hands trembled when she reached out for the tempting delight he offered.

Her nails grazed his shaft, smearing the pre-cum over her fingertips. When she closed her hand around his cock though, she held nothing but air.

She spun around quickly, bewildered. Tristan stood a few steps to her left, his hand sliding up and down his rod, stretching the skin taut along the thick length.

"Now that I have your undivided attention," he said, that cocky grin she'd come to recognize lighting up his face, "I thought we could talk."

"You're an asshole, you know that, Chance?"

Tristan chuckled and held up his hands in supplication. "I just want to talk."

Lara crossed her arms beneath her breasts, the movement stretching the material of her gossamer-thin top over her perky breasts. Tonight, she wore a see-through gray blouse that showed off a black bra and her flat stomach to cock-hardening perfection. Her skirt rode low on her hips, reaching to mid-thigh and flaring slightly at the bottom. Strappy sandals and a thin gold belt completed the ensemble.

"Then you shouldn't have touched me first," she snapped. Her nipples puckered into hard little beads and pressed against her bra.

"Fuck, you're gorgeous when you're angry."

It wasn't the right thing to say, but he didn't give a damn. Lara shook her head in a gesture of exasperation and annoyance. Her eyes were so dark they looked almost black, a startling contrast to the soft streams of moonlight that streaked her riot of ringlets with silver thread.

She hadn't bothered to smooth down her skirt, Tristan noticed with an absurdly pleased grin, and he had a perfect view of her smooth mound, slicked with her juices and his saliva.

He could still taste her on his lips. The spicy flavor of her arousal lingered in his mouth like an aphrodisiac, the aroma filling his senses with pounding, raging need for her.

Damn. Talking had seemed like a good idea at the time.

Tristan slid his hand up the length of his cock and smoothed his palm over the tip, rubbing at the pounding ache that had settled there. "There are some things you need to know."

Her brow furrowed but he noticed she didn't take her eyes off his dick. That was encouraging at least.

"You broke your part of the bargain," she said. "I see no problem with breaking mine." Her hand drifted over her stomach to dip between her legs. She met his gaze, daring him to stop her.

Tristan gritted his teeth. He was almost certain that if he didn't make her come directly, the curse wouldn't take over.

But *almost* certain wouldn't cut it. Before she came again while he was near, he had to spell out the risks. She had a right to know what they were up against—what *she* was up against.

He moved to stand behind her, so fast he barely disturbed the air between them. She gasped as he grabbed her wrists and brought her hands behind her back.

"Nuh-uh," he admonished gently in her ear. "Not yet."

"How do you do that?" Wonder filled her breathy whisper.

He tugged her close and wrapped her in his arms. Her body stiffened and for a moment he feared she'd yank free of his grasp. When she relaxed against him, he couldn't help the sigh that ripped from his throat.

"I'm not like you, Lara," he murmured, pushing her hair aside with one hand and leaning in to kiss the soft skin of her neck. Her honeyed, feminine scent blended with the fragrance of eucalyptus stirred by the breeze. Each beat of her heart thrummed through him, lighting a blazing heat in his veins, rousing a need he couldn't deny.

"What does that mean?"

"It means there are some things you need to know about me. About us."

She attempted a laugh. "He warned me about you."

"Your father?"

Lara nodded. "My brother too. Were they right, Tristan? Are you as dangerous as they say you are?"

He slid his hand over her breast, pausing to sweep his thumb over a hard nipple then flicked the topmost button of her blouse open. "I'm not privy to the conversations that go on behind my back." Another button followed then another. "But yes, I think it's safe to say that whatever your father told you is at least based in truth."

She swallowed hard. Her pulse sped, the rush of her blood streaming through her veins growing as loud as the crashing surf. The sounds rang through Tristan's head, elongating his fangs. If he hadn't already fed tonight, he wasn't sure he could hold back the beast within. The constant, aching hunger that ruled his life demanded to be fed with every pounding beat of Lara's heart.

"I shouldn't be here," Lara whispered.

Tristan released her hands and slid her blouse over her shoulders then trailed his lips over the smooth pale skin he uncovered. "You're probably right."

A sound that could have been a whimper or a shadow of a protest escaped her throat but she made no move to stop him. He unclasped her bra and watched it fall, black against the glittering grains of golden sand.

The froth of the incoming waves slid across the surface of the beach, teasing his bare feet, dipping inside Lara's sandals. She shivered, but whether from the feel of the cold water or from his touch, he couldn't tell. He hoped it was the latter.

He tugged on the zipper holding her skirt tight across her small waist then watched it fall in the waves that crept closer with each surging ripple of foam.

She finally stood before him, nude but for the sandals she still wore. His cock pressed against the curve of her spine, nestled in the heat emanating from her body.

I should go. I should pull away. I should –

"Oh!"

As Lara's doubt ran through his mind, both of Tristan's hands moved with incredible speed. One slipped between her inner thighs, finding the moist heat of her pussy. The other tweaked a nipple hard between thumb and forefinger.

"You are in danger," he whispered in her ear, his knuckle grazing her clit. "But not from me." He grimaced. "Not directly anyway."

She writhed against him, her ass rubbing up and down against his skin as she wiggled her clit closer to his hand. Tristan's cock swelled until he feared he'd spill his seed on her back. That wasn't what he wanted for them tonight. He needed to lose himself in her, to forget at least for a while that her life depended on his ability to keep her safe. And to do that, he had to put a stop to this curse.

"I don't understand." The words came out on a gasp. He slid two fingers inside her pussy and her inner muscles clenched, holding him tight. He pulled on her nipple until she hissed.

Her arousal flooded his mind, her lust overcoming his self-control. He had to tell her. Reason screamed at him to pull away, to pin her on the ground if he had to and make her understand.

But his body had other plans.

"Listen to me." He trailed the tip of one fang over her neck. Lara cried out, a thin, sharp sound. He pressed his thumb against her clit and her cry turned into a moan.

A thin trickle of blood ran down her pale skin, glistening in the moonlight. He licked it off, sealing the wound. "I need you. But if I fuck you, you're going to run."

"I'm not," she protested, her voice husky with need. "I want—"

"I know you do." He kissed her collarbone and fought the urge to scrape her skin with his teeth. "But it's not up to you. There are forces at play that you just don't understand."

She spun around in his arms, her finger jabbing his shoulder. "Don't treat me like a child. I'm not stupid, and whether you want to believe it or not, I'm in full control of my emotions."

Tristan shook his head. Fury blazed in her eyes, her angry gaze piercing his soul. He wished he could make her understand, but to do that he'd have to explain everything, from the nature of his being to the magical origins of the curse. Would she accept what he told her? Or would she run anyway, this time thinking him a lunatic?

"I know this is difficult," he began, but she cut him off by pressing two fingers against his lips.

"Actually, it's really easy." She slid her hand between them to cradle his balls in her hand. She stepped forward, trapping his shaft between their bodies. When she bent her head and nipped his nipple in her teeth, a tremor ran down his body. His cock pulsed and pounded in delicious agony.

"Lara." He'd meant the word to be a warning, but it came out deep and husky, filled with the overwhelming lust that dripped through every inch of him.

She straightened to her full height. Her breasts pressed against his chest, her tightly beaded nipples grazing his skin, sending tingles of arousal into his already aching groin.

"Enough." She stood on the tips of her toes and wrapped her arms around his neck. Her breath warmed his lips when she spoke. "I ran the other night but I won't run again. I haven't been sleeping well and the intensity of what I felt for you must have scared me. It won't happen again."

He swallowed hard, wishing that were true.

She quirked a perfectly arched eyebrow. "You don't believe me."

"It's just that—"

"Then let me show you." She grabbed his hand and led him a few steps away from the surf, where he'd laid his jacket earlier.

She released him and lowered herself to the ground, her gaze never leaving his. She stretched her long legs in front of her, giving him a perfect view of the dewy folds of her pussy. Even the moonlight seemed to be conspiring against him as it pooled the light between her legs, the moisture there glistening, inviting him to kneel and have another taste.

Tristan groaned and tightened his hands into fists at his sides, fighting for control. He'd always prided himself on keeping the upper hand despite any temptation that came his way and in the past it had been easy.

Women were easy.

But not Lara. She was a wonderful contradiction of strength and vulnerability. Her ability to stand up to him both bewildered and aroused him. He'd known she wanted him, but he hadn't expected her to be so adamant about her needs. The fact that she could lie before him naked, completely unashamed of her nudity, drove him insane. He knew she'd had enough practice showing her body to strangers but this felt different, as though she were offering him a priceless gift.

And God help him, he knew he wouldn't be able to turn it down.

Lara leaned back, holding her weight on her elbows. She drew her heels up close to the plump curve of her ass. Her thighs were open, zooming his gaze on her soaked flesh.

"Fuck me, Tristan."

A growl broke free from his throat as his self-restraint shattered. He fell to his knees and fit his body perfectly within the space she offered, his cock laying flat against her pussy. His upper body followed, his torso slamming down on top of her. He'd moved too fast without meaning to and a sharp breath escaped her lungs.

He cupped her face in his hands and kissed her full lips, sliding his tongue between them to taste the heat of her mouth. She groaned and he absorbed the sound, moving his hips and positioning the tip of his cock at her entrance.

"If we do this," he whispered against her mouth, "you have to promise me you'll fight the urge to run." He began to move, his cock sliding inside her soaked channel bit by torturous bit. Her velvet heat held him prisoner, tugging at his restraint until he thought he'd explode inside her before they even began. "Fight it with every ounce of self-control you possess."

Lara whimpered, thrusting her hips upward to impale herself on his shaft. Her cunt muscles quivered as they adjusted to the intrusion. She gasped, the sound impossibly loud until he realized the air had gone still around them. The hard drumming of her heart and the blood rushing through her body filled his senses, drowning out every other sound, enveloping him in lust and hot, dark heat.

Lara dug her nails into his shoulders. "Don't tell me what to do," she murmured, thrusting upward again, impaling herself fully on his cock. Her sleek curves molded to his much larger frame, the silky feel of her body sending a spike of adrenaline through his.

Unable to hold back any longer, he drove into her hard, watching as her eyes drifted closed and her mouth parted. Color washed over her cheeks and small, breathless moans escaped her lips.

His knees slipped on the jacket's liner until the material slid upward and his flesh scraped against the cold, hard sand. He didn't care. The stinging discomfort was nothing compared to the burning pleasure stroking his cock.

"You're close." It wasn't a question. He could feel it through the unexplainable bond they shared. Desire glided along his every nerve ending and he knew the fog of lust clouding his senses wasn't entirely his own.

"Yes." Lara's hoarse, needy whisper sent a jolt to his cock. Her eyelashes fluttered and she met his gaze boldly, her hips writhing against his, her cunt tightening around him, milking him with every small tremble of her body.

He palmed her breast with one hand, tweaking a nipple between his fingers. He couldn't stop the rush of orgasm that would inevitably hit both of them, but he could do everything in his power to make sure she didn't run.

And then there was no more time for words or contemplation.

The hunger took over and he drove his fangs into her neck as she cried out, wrapping her legs around his waist, holding him close while wave after wave of unabashed pleasure washed over them both.

The sensation was too much. Lara's muscles spasmed and her blood rushed down Tristan's throat with an intensity that exploded inside him. His balls drew tight in his sac in that familiar climb toward orgasm. In a flash, he lost himself in her delicious burning heat. His cock quivered, pulsing with the release of his seed as it spilled inside her, drenching her inner core.

Dizziness hit Tristan like a punch to the jaw. He slid his fangs from Lara's sweet flesh and licked the wound to close it then shut his eyes tightly against the nauseating motion of the rapidly spinning beach.

The effects of too much blood drunk too quickly mingled with the impact of Tristan's release, sending pulsing tremors through his overheated body. His muscles clenched and unclenched as a deluge of new blood poured through his veins.

Through an intoxicated daze, he registered Lara's palms pressing hard against his chest. Vaguely aware that his entire weight bore down on her slender body, he rolled off her and onto his back, the contented afterglow of orgasm still sweeping through him.

"I'm sorry if I hurt you." His voice was hoarse, as if he hadn't used it in much too long.

Cold water splashed over his feet, trickling between his toes. The startling contrast of ice-cold surf against his burning skin sent a shiver through his body. He turned on his side and reached for Lara but found only empty air.

"Oh fuck!"

A spike of adrenaline jolted him to his feet just in time to catch sight of Lara's shapely and very naked ass disappearing between the tall trunks of two palm trees.

Chapter Eight

Terror closed in on Lara, enveloping her in a cocoon of fear. It slid along her skin, pressing in on her from all sides, urging her feet to keep moving. Her thoughts slipped through her brain like streams of mercury, impossible to catch. Somewhere in the darkest corner of her mind, a part of her was screaming, but she couldn't isolate it enough to figure out why it mattered.

She rounded a corner and slammed into a parked car. Instinctively, she reached out to steady herself, her sweaty palms leaving imprints in the dust and grime layered over the navy blue Ford.

Her throat choked with dread. For a moment, her knees buckled and she used the rear bumper to steady herself. The streets were empty, with the exception of a woman walking a poodle. They were still too far away to have noticed her, but they would soon.

I can't stay here. He'll find me.

The irrational thought was the first coherent one she'd had since she took off from the beach and she was grateful for it, no matter how sudden or unexpected. Her legs obeyed and a moment later she was running past a neat row of brightly colored flowers, past a white picket fence, past a swing set.

She flew down the street, her surroundings blending into a blur of indistinct shapes. The moon had dropped lower in the black sky where it hung like a medallion among a gaggle of bright stars.

The woman with the dog gaped as Lara neared, her paper-thin liver-spotted skin stretched tight over high cheekbones. "Are you okay, dear?" she asked.

Lara kept moving. Her heart had leapt into her throat and remained there, beating hard enough to choke her. Blood roared in her ears.

He's close.

She could feel him trailing her, like a shadow she couldn't escape. A thrumming ache settled low in her belly at the thought of him—a sharp, pleasant and altogether puzzling contrast to the cramp in her side.

She couldn't think, couldn't recall why she had to keep running, what this man had done to her. He was dangerous, yes, that much she remembered. But why?

That she didn't know. She knew only that if she stopped, she'd die.

Dark shapes in the distance drew her attention as she skidded around another corner, turning on to a side road away from the beach. She could make out about half a dozen men, standing around in a circle, their laughter piercing the otherwise quiet street.

Teenagers? Possibly. Or worse.

Every last part of her that still answered to reason cried out for her to stop, to turn around and run the way she'd come. Her feet wouldn't listen. Adrenaline pumped through her veins and she forced herself to slow but it was too late. They'd already seen her.

The chuckles died, dissipating on the warm breeze. She couldn't make out their features in the dark but the purposeful gait with which they strode toward her made their determination clear.

A squeak escaped her throat. She cast a frenzied glance to her left but found her way blocked by a tall metal gate. To her right, she could see the edges of a well-maintained cemetery.

A low growl resonated in her ear and she knew she'd run out of time. He'd found her.

Though the driving panic sweeping through her urged her to do nothing more but curl into a ball and hide, she spun and sprinted toward the cemetery. She'd only taken a few steps before strong arms encircled her waist and she felt her feet leave the ground.

"Let me go!" Her cry echoed down the street but she knew no one would come to her aid. The men hadn't stopped advancing but they were out of her line of sight in the span of time it had taken her heart to drum another beat.

Lara fought the iron grip that held her prisoner. She banged her fists against the massive chest, her skin rippling with need as it made contact with the man's flesh. She could feel the smooth play of muscle under skin and the sensation fanned the flame searing her cunt. Worse yet, in his arms she felt weightless and...*safe*. Turning her attack into a caress was much too tempting.

And much too dangerous.

Again that growl low in her ear, as though he wanted to say something, perhaps a million somethings, but held back. She could feel his anger, his frustration, his worry. They all blended with one another and merged with her own feelings, adding to the relentless war that waged inside her.

Terror swam in her mind, flooding her senses. Lara had a vivid image of herself as a fly trapped in amber, except her prison had no physical form. It was of her own making and lived solely inside her head.

If she could make sense of that much, surely she could put an end to the endless fright driving her persistent need to flee?

"I'm going to put you down now," he said, and for the first time Lara realized they'd stopped moving.

They stood beside the sleek wall of an elegant crypt. Vines snaked up its length, spiraling upward toward the sky. Around them, tombstones marked the permanent resting place of a hundred people. The scent of freshly dug earth teased her nostrils.

If she hadn't already been terrified, her surroundings would certainly have driven her wild with fear. The moon had disappeared, as though even it wouldn't cast its silvery light upon this ghoulish place.

"We'll be safe here." The man's voice was soothing. A pang of recognition slammed into Lara's belly, penetrating the fear for only a moment before it once again took over. "It's probably the only place on this entire island where no one is likely to come upon a naked woman at this hour."

True to his word, he set her down. Her feet slid into soft grass, the dewy moisture slicking her toes through the open gap in her sandals. She tried not to think about the horrors that lay in wait beneath the lush, inviting turf.

Knowing she wouldn't get another chance, she took advantage of the shift in his stance to lunge forward, making a mad dash around him. His arm shot out quicker than she could see it move, halting her progress. In another instant, she was trapped against him, his solid body pressing into her back.

His erection nudged her spine, sending a gush of cream to her pussy. The tip of Lara's tongue snaked out and she tasted the salt on her lip. Had she been crying? She couldn't remember. She swept the back of her hand over one cheek and it came away wet.

"Shhh," he soothed in a calm, even voice. "It's my fault. I should have explained everything to you before we made love."

His words sent a ripple of need down her belly. Raw, hot excitement permeated her bloodstream.

Memories slammed into her brain, a dozen images, sounds and scents infusing her mind with sensory overload. She remembered the weight of his body on top of her, his masculine form pressing against her breasts, her stomach, her thighs. She could still feel his cock nudging its way inside her, parting the folds of her pussy and stretching her wide as it thrust into her wet, waiting channel. His mouth had tasted of wine and metal, a familiar flavor she couldn't place. He'd smelled of the ocean, of lust and arousal, of her own cream that still lingered on his lips.

As abruptly as it started, the flow of sensation came to a stop. Only one memory persisted. It was a clear picture of Lara in this man's arms, melding physically to him. Her head was thrown back as he fucked her, her lips parted as though she'd just whispered his name and now it hung frozen in the air like a ghostly reminder of a past life.

"Dear God." Her breath hitched on the words. "What's happening to me?"

The arms that held her captive released her. With inhuman speed, the man moved to stand in front of her and gripped her upper arms, the solid hold bordering on pain.

Inhuman.

The word lingered in her brain, resonating with importance. Lara clenched her teeth. Despite the fear that clenched her gut, she looked up.

And for a moment, she forgot the terror seeping through her veins. Hell, for a moment, she forgot to *breathe.*

His muscular form blocked out the night—a shadow within shadows. She could make out impressively broad shoulders and the lean lines of his body. His chest was bare as were his legs, but she'd felt the silky softness of his boxers when he'd pressed up against her.

But his eyes...oh God, his green eyes gleamed with golden fire in the inky blackness.

Lara tried desperately to cling to any pale shred of control she could grasp. If she panicked, the darkness would overcome her completely. Already her knees buckled and she trembled. Only his firm grasp on her arms held her upright.

"Lara, listen to me," he said. "You're in a danger. I'm not what you think I am but you've figured that out already, haven't you?"

She licked her dry lips. Instinctively, she tried to take a step back but his steadfast hold kept her rooted to the spot.

"My true nature is known to only a few and I wouldn't be sharing it with you now if it wasn't important. I'm going to trust you with my deepest secret. Do you understand?"

She swallowed hard. His words made little sense when accompanied by the frenzied pounding of her heart. Still, she nodded.

"Good." He took a deep breath, the burning embers in his gaze dying for a moment while his eyelids drifted closed. "I am—"

A deafening clap flooded the silent cemetery then another and another. The sounds drifted close to Lara's ear, like the rapid beat of impending thunder ringing perilously close.

Lara reeled back, suddenly unrestrained. She lost her footing and landed hard on the grass. A stab of pain ran up her elbow. Cool, wet earth clung to her skin.

Her captor swore, his voice breaking on the expletive. He stumbled backward, his upper body wrenching sideways and slamming against the surface of the crypt.

Lara didn't understand what just happened but her terror-stricken mind wrapped around one fact and desperately clung to the sliver of hope it brought—she was free.

She scrambled to her feet. No longer caring whether Tristan would follow, Lara broke into a mad dash for the edge of the cemetery.

Tristan.

His name slammed into the deepest recesses of her mind a second time, bringing her legs to a stumbling halt. Her toes tangled in a wreath someone had laid at the base of a headstone and she reached out to steady herself by grasping the cool marble.

The fog that had draped over Lara began to lift. She spun around, her heart beating wildly, this time with genuine dread as her mind made sense of the sound she'd heard.

Tristan had been shot.

* * * * *

"Run!"

The cry tore from Tristan's throat even as another bullet zipped by his ear. His hyperaware senses flared, attuned to the slightest sound. The advance warning he'd gain from hearing the trigger being pulled and the bullet released wouldn't help him much in his current state, but it was better than nothing.

Blood poured from his shoulder, warm and wet, slicking his chest. Pain flared and traveled down the length of his arm. He gritted his teeth against the agony, trying to ignore the burning sting with little success. His skin felt as though it had been doused with pure sunlight and was even now dissipating like mist before the unforgiving rays of the sun.

His gaze slid across the graveyard, looking for his attacker. In the dark, his night sight could pick up the slightest trace of body heat, drawing a clear outline around any shape. He saw no one but Lara, who stood rooted to the ground, her body still and tense.

"Fuck," Tristan murmured. A few minutes ago, he couldn't get her to stop running. Now that he wanted her to go, she wouldn't move.

Figured.

He rushed toward the gravestone and caught her wrist, pulling her as he dashed past. "We have to get out of here."

Lara stumbled but quickly matched his pace. Having lost so much blood, Tristan couldn't use his supernatural speed to get them out of there. He willed his feet to move, though the agony in his shoulder made him grit his teeth with each stride.

Another bang echoed in the still darkness.

Lara screamed. "Someone's shooting at us!"

"That would explain why we're running." Pain slammed into his shoulder as he yanked on her wrist to ensure she stayed close to him then leapt over the last patch of grass and landed on the sidewalk.

They ran, past the row of well-manicured lawns, past the parked cars idling in perfectly symmetrical driveways, past tall palm trees that silently watched their progression, leaves swaying in the predawn breeze.

Tristan led them down side streets as he fought to stay out of populated areas. A naked woman and a bleeding man were bound to attract attention. The gunfire had stopped as soon as they'd left the cemetery but he remained wary, his senses on high alert.

The fact that he hadn't been able to see or hear his attacker before the bullet hit home made his gut clench. Had he been so distracted by Lara that he hadn't been able to discern they were no longer alone?

He clenched his jaw as the iron gates of Hayden's mansion came into view. Blackness swam behind his eyes, threatening to drown him as pain flooded every inch of his body. His flesh burned, the torment searing into his bones. Only Lara's rapidly pounding heart and the rhythmic thrumming of their feet hitting the concrete kept him moving.

He glanced up at the stone gargoyles and the gates swung open with a loud metal groan. He didn't dare slow down even once they were inside and running up the winding path, knowing that if he did, he'd collapse. Only a steady stream of adrenaline stood between him and utter darkness, the complete oblivion his spent body would welcome.

Bright white light spilled from the multitude of windows, shining like a beacon in eternal darkness. As they neared, Hayden pulled the door open, his face drawn into a tight grimace.

He ran down the few steps to meet them and Tristan allowed himself to slump into his brother's arms.

"Can't leave you alone for a minute, can I?" Hayden's grave tone betrayed his playful words.

"Who — who are you?" Lara asked.

Tristan stumbled over his feet, Hayden supporting most of his weight as they climbed up the stairs and stepped over the threshold inside the hallway. The door slammed closed behind them.

"Hayden Chance. I'd ask who you are but under the circumstances, I'm afraid I already know."

How? Why? What's going on?

A torrent of questions flooded Tristan's mind but Lara only voiced one aloud. "Is he going to be okay?"

Tristan yearned to reassure her but his lips wouldn't move. His eyelids drifted closed. He struggled in vain to open them, fighting against the oppressive weight that kept them firmly shut.

Hayden loosened his hold and Tristan's body sank into a soft, welcoming surface.

"I'm going to make damn sure of that."

You're going to be okay. I promise you.

Hayden's words echoed in Tristan's mind, blending with Lara's endless questions. Their thoughts merged in his head, a welcoming duet of familiarity that tugged at Tristan's soul.

Deep within oblivion beckoned, teasing him with the promise of eternal night. Lara's inner turmoil shifted, her confusion turning into a stream of prayer. She called on a deity Tristan no longer believed in but that didn't matter because she had enough faith for both of them.

Then even that stopped, her terror once again ramming into him like a physical force.

"Drink, brother. Let the blood of our line close your wounds." Hayden held his wrist to Tristan's mouth, forcing his lips open. "Drink."

He saw himself through Lara's eyes, his mouth clamped greedily around his brother's flesh, sucking at the tear Hayden had ripped in his vein.

Blood coated Tristan's raw throat, flooding his mouth with potent flavor. It rushed through his body, tensing his muscles, hardening his cock, mending the shredded flesh with a rush of powerful fury. It pushed the bullet from his shoulder and he heard it fall onto the floor with a faint metallic clang as it hit the flat surface of the rug.

Lara tried to stifle a scream but only partly succeeded. Tristan felt her fear as though it were his own, heard her tired mind's panicked thoughts as she tried to make sense of the scene unfolding before her.

At long last, Hayden gently pulled his wrist away. Tristan blinked his eyes open, his gaze falling on Lara. He'd grown so damn accustomed to seeing terror in her eyes. Until this moment, he'd known it to be the effect of the curse. Now though, she stared at him in open wonder, her dark eyes wide, her hand clamped to her mouth.

"What—what *are* you?"

The undisguised dismay flickering across her features hurt more than all the wounds bullets could inflict. He grimaced and raised himself up to a sitting position.

Hayden saved him the trouble of finding a suitable response where none existed. "Vampires. Vampyrs. The undead."

Lara's eyebrows drew together and she took a deep, shuddering breath. "I should have known." She trailed her fingertips across the tender skin at the side of her neck.

"You had no reason to believe our kind even existed," Tristan said.

She leveled a flat gaze at him. "The marks on my neck. The way you move. The way your eyes flicker from within as though lit by an otherworldly force. And those things my father said in the boardroom... I should have known," she repeated.

He felt the tension ebb from her shoulders. She slumped into a nearby chair, kicked off her mud-covered sandals and drew her feet up under her. Though she remained naked, her nudity didn't seem to concern her at all.

He remembered the way she looked, sprawled across the table at Bitter Sweet, dozens of eyes drinking in the full curves of her breasts, the tender folds of her pink, succulent pussy.

His cock stiffened farther, tenting the boxers he wore. He looked down to find blood smeared across his chest and grimaced, realizing what he must look like to her. Everything about her embodied seduction, the sinful temptation of human nature. And everything about him screamed monster, the immortal representation of the beast within.

Tristan blew out a breath and leaned forward. "There's more."

The tip of her tongue slipped out between her lips to moisten them. "Relax. I won't run again." She tilted her head to the side and watched him with a gaze no longer clouded by fear.

Admiration swept through Tristan. Not many women could witness what she had and still remain in the room, willing to talk.

But Lara wasn't like other women. He'd known that from the moment he'd laid eyes on her. She was strong yet vulnerable. Intelligent yet with an endearing naïveté that both aroused and intrigued him.

And she was his.

"You were right when you said I was dangerous but not for the reasons you think."

He waited for a response. When one didn't come, he continued. "My bloodline is cursed."

Lara arched an eyebrow. "Cursed," she repeated.

Hayden perched on the edge of the sofa. Earlier it had been cream-colored. Now Tristan's blood turned the pale color a dark shade of crimson.

"He's telling the truth. Every male member of the Chance family is plagued by this magic."

Lara shook her head. "I don't understand what that has to do with me. I'm not a Chance." Her lips quirked upward. "And I'm not male."

Tristan stared at her breasts, at the dusky tips that hardened as she spoke. "You're certainly not," he agreed.

"The curse affects our mates as much as it affects us," Hayden supplied. "It ensures we can never have the one woman we desire above all else."

Color crept into her cheeks. She ran her hand through her curls, leaving the riot of ringlets disheveled in its wake. "You mean I'm…"

"My mate," Tristan supplied. He steepled his hands in front of him. "Trust me, I found this whole thing unbelievable too."

A laugh escaped her throat, silvery and altogether too tempting. "This is absurd."

"Is it?" Hayden moved to stand beside her chair so she had to look up at him. "Then why do you run every time Tristan brings you to climax?"

Her flush deepened. She lowered her gaze and grasped her lower lip between her teeth. "I don't know," she whispered.

"I do," Tristan said. "The curse takes over. It overwhelms you, strips of your free will and drives you as far away from me as quickly as possible."

Is that also why when you're around, I can't keep from touching you?

The intimacy of the thought made a groan break free from Tristan's throat. Lara looked up sharply.

"Ah, yes…and I think the curse allows me to know your thoughts."

She gaped at him. "You can read my mind?"

Hayden chuckled. "From what I've observed, the ability is unreliable at best. It seems to only work with intense thoughts. Fear. Lust. Anger. That sort of thing."

Lara rubbed the bridge of her nose. "What else can you do? Shift into a bat? Turn into mist and slide through keyholes?"

Tristan grinned. "You've been watching too many late-night movies. No, we can't shapeshift into bats or anything else. In fact, most of the vampire myths of today are just that. Myths." He pointed to the glass wall where his distorted form shimmered. "I have a reflection. Garlic only makes me wrinkle my nose at the stench. As for the whole cross thing, well, the one Hayden's worn for centuries hasn't affected him in any negative way, so I'd say we're safe there."

She rubbed her fingertips over the bite marks on her throat that had all but faded from sight. "The blood drinking is real, isn't it?"

He licked his suddenly dry lips. "It is. We need blood to survive, just as you need human food. The plasma sustains us."

Lara paled. "How much do you take?"

His heart clenched at the way her voice quivered slightly. He ached to reassure her. "I'd never hurt you, Lara. Never. As vampires, our existence depends on obtaining what we can't naturally produce. I don't have enough blood running through my system, so I need a willing donor." He cringed at the hypocrisy of using that word when he'd chastised Hayden for depending on Illiana to meet his needs.

Still, *donor* sounded so much better than *victim*, and the last thing he wanted to do was scare Lara any further.

Lara's gaze slid between Hayden and Tristan. "You became vampires at the same time?"

Hayden nodded. "It was all Alexander's fault. That boy's fascination with vampires began long before any of us had ever heard the word. He fancied himself a slayer and went looking for trouble."

"We went with him," Tristan said, a smile lifting the corners of his mouth. They'd been so young then, so naïve about the way the world worked. "Our brother was so taken with tales of evil creatures, we didn't have the heart to tell him such things didn't exist."

Lara released a shuddering breath. "But they did exist. You found one, didn't you?"

"He found us," Hayden said. "And he wasn't alone."

Murky, long-forgotten bursts of memories flickered across Tristan's mind. The night his life had changed forever had always been hazy. He remembered scents and sounds vividly but images eluded him. He couldn't even call up a picture of the man who'd turned him, despite the intimacy of the act. But he recalled his brothers' voices, the scent and taste of their blood, and the way they'd drawn strength from one another. That was enough.

"We were turned in a cemetery much like the one you and I visited tonight," Tristan said. "Alexander had followed the beast to his lair and we came along for the ride, thinking we'd give him a good scare and then spend the rest of the evening in a tavern somewhere."

"Brothers," Lara murmured. "They're a pain in the ass."

Hayden threw his head back and laughed, a hearty sound that bounced off the glass walls. Tristan responded despite himself and soon they were both shaking with mirth. "Ain't that the truth. Even when they're three hundred years old."

Lara shuddered visibly. "Three hundred years shackled to the same family. I can't even imagine such a thing."

"We're very fortunate," Tristan said, glancing at Hayden. "We've always been close. The vampires who turned us abandoned us that same night and we had no one to lean on but each other. The only way to learn what we were and how to survive was through trial and error."

Hayden's grin faded. "There were too many errors for my liking, especially during the first few years."

"But you survived," Lara pointed out. "And Alexander?"

"He's as headstrong as ever. Lives in London now and doesn't have much use for his older and overprotective brothers."

Lara frowned, her eyes narrowing. "There's so much to learn about you, about your family. Yet I have the feeling you're holding something back. Is there anything else I should know?"

Tristan shot a glance at his brother.

It's up to you how much you reveal. She doesn't need to know all the details.

Tristan frowned. *Like hell she doesn't.*

Hayden lifted his shoulders in a half shrug.

"What is it?" Lara asked, looking from one to the other. "What aren't you telling me?"

"The family curse I mentioned comes with a deadline." Tristan stood and crossed the distance between them, needing to be close to her when she learned the truth. He kneeled before her and took both hands in his. "We have to find a cure in less than four days."

She swallowed hard then peered at him intently. "Or what?"

"Or you die."

Her face drained of color. Shock registered in her eyes then denial then anger in quick succession. "Why are you doing this?"

He squeezed her hands. "Because you need to know. And we need to stop this."

"Fine." She pulled out of his grasp and rose to her feet. "Then let's stop it."

Hayden crossed the length of the room, stopping in front of a window. Before him, the ocean stretched out, the first pink highlights of dawn streaking the horizon. "We don't know how."

For a moment, Tristan wasn't sure whether Lara had heard his brother's words. Then she threw her hands up in the air and he knew she understood.

"This just gets better and better, doesn't it?"

Tristan trailed his fingertips up her inner thigh. His face was level with her pussy, and her arousal dominated his senses. "We'll find a way to end it, Lara. I promise."

She shuddered under his touch. "Oh yeah? And how do you plan to do that?"

"We know that the woman who originally cast the curse has descendants living right here on the island."

She looked skeptical. "And they know what to do?"

"No," Hayden said, not turning around. His reflection stared back at them from the full-length window. "I questioned Illiana again after you left. She doesn't know a thing about curses, whether cast by her ancestor or not. And although she has a brother—"

"Great. I'll go see him," Tristan said.

Hayden scrubbed a hand over his face. "Good luck. I've already spoken to him too. If possible, he knows even less about the occult than his sister."

"Illiana knows about us," Tristan said. "I assume she didn't faint when you told her so she must know something about the supernatural."

"Only that it exists and at times it comes with pleasurable benefits."

Lara stiffened. "I really don't need to hear this."

Hayden spun around, his hands clasped behind his back, a sly smile playing across his features. "Dawn is minutes away. I suggest we all sleep on this. Perhaps a solution will present itself."

"The sunlight myth. That's real too, isn't it?"

Tristan grimaced. "Of all the silly superstitious ideas people have about us, that's the one I wish they'd gotten wrong. Yes, sunlight is lethal to vampires. In fact, it's the simplest and most direct method of destroying us." He swallowed hard as old sorrows pushed their way through the barrier he'd erected around his heart, threatening to overwhelm him. "And it's the surest means we have to kill ourselves."

Lara glanced toward the door. "We can meet after sunset tomorrow then. If you'll lend me some clothes, I'll call a cab. I have a suite at the hotel."

Tristan shook his head and rose. "You're not going anywhere. Not with an assassin on the loose."

Lara frowned. "What makes you think he was after me?"

"He wasn't." Tristan eyed the bullet that had been in his shoulder and now lay harmlessly on the floor. "It's silver. Whoever shot at us had damn good aim. He wanted me."

"Oh."

You could have been killed.

She didn't say the words but he saw the fear etched across her features as she contemplated that dire truth.

"Yes. But I wasn't."

She took a deep breath. "Because Hayden healed you."

"We can't heal ourselves but we can heal others. That's why the incisions I made when I drank from you closed so quickly."

She clenched and unclenched her fists at her sides. "I still don't understand why I can't leave. If the assassin wasn't after me—"

"We can't be sure of that. Just because the bullet was meant for me doesn't mean this guy won't use you to get what he wants." Tristan caressed her cheek with the back of his hand. "I can't risk it, sweetheart."

He saw the indecision warring within her, heard it as it flooded her thoughts. At long last she nodded. "I'll stay. Until we find a way to end the curse."

"And we will end the curse, Lara. I swear it."

She tilted her head, her gaze boring into his. He felt the panic ebb from her thoughts. It wasn't the reluctant acceptance of a woman who knew her fate and met it head on, but the hopeful faith of someone who wholeheartedly believed in something.

"I know," she whispered.

The confidence she placed in him made his heart clench but it was the words she didn't say that startled him the most.

I trust you.

Tristan's mind reeled. He was used to being respected, obeyed, even feared. But trusted? That required a level of conviction he rarely inspired.

He slid his hand into hers. The contact of her warm skin against his flesh sent a ripple of need through his body. His gut clenched with the sudden and unshakable realization that he couldn't let her go. Not tonight—not ever.

Now that he'd finally admitted to himself he'd found his mate, he knew he'd never be able to watch her walk away. And he had four days to convince her that she needed him as much as he needed her.

Together they followed Hayden, who lifted the wooden hatch and led them down a narrow set of stairs. Candles ensconced at regular intervals in the walls lit their path down a shadowy corridor. Wooden doors with gleaming golden handles marked at least half a dozen rooms on each side.

Hayden stopped in front of one and opened it then gestured inside. "The main guest room. I'm afraid I was only expecting one guest but the bed is big enough for two. There's a bathroom across the hall. You're welcome to use it to clean up. None of the doors are locked."

Tristan glanced down at the dried blood covering his chest and grimaced. He slid his hand out of Lara's then placed a quick kiss on her temple. "I'll be back in a moment."

The nourishment he'd taken from his brother surged through his veins, driving his ability to speed his movements. He practically flew through the bathroom, barely taking in the lush marble décor. Rivulets of water still ran down his skin when he returned, but at least he was no longer covered in gore.

He reached Lara's side in time to see Hayden disappear into a room two doors down from theirs. Lara blinked rapidly and shook her head. "I don't know if I'll ever get used to that. You were only gone for a few moments."

Tristan lifted a shoulder in a half shrug. "I couldn't bear to be away from you any longer than necessary."

A rosy blush crept up Lara's cheeks. "My turn. You'll wait for me before heading to bed?"

Her words were simple enough, but her expression did him in. Longing and need flickered in her gaze and he yearned to wrap his arms around her and reassure her. After the evening she'd had, she could use all the comfort her had to offer.

He pushed a messy curl behind her ear and nodded. "Take your time. I'll be right here when you're ready for me."

She glanced over his shoulder toward the bedroom. "I'll hold you to that."

Tristan watched as she headed for the bathroom and closed the door softly behind her. He considered going inside and making himself comfortable, but a nagging feeling at the back of his mind warned him she might try to leave. He wasn't about to let that happen.

Instead of entering the bedroom, Tristan leaned against the wall in the hallway and waited. He heard the shower run and closed his eyes, picturing her body glistening wetly beneath the streaming jet.

When she came out, he was breathing hard. He rubbed the heel of his palm against his aching cock.

She halted in mid-stride, her eyes widening when she caught sight of him. "I didn't mean you couldn't go ahead without me." She rubbed the ends of her locks with a white towel, squeezing out the moisture. She hadn't bothered to wrap a second towel around herself and the sight of her, naked and completely unashamed, sent a jolt of lust to burrow deep in his balls.

Tristan grabbed Lara's hand and yanked her after him. The towel dropped to the floor as the bedroom door slammed shut behind them.

At first glance the room looked simple, decorated with the same modern-style furniture that lined Hayden's main floor. A low coffee table and a metal bookshelf sat against the far wall. Candlelight flooded a king-sized bed, drifting across the black sheets and gleaming off the surface of a massive wooden chest that sat at the foot of the bed.

The lid gaped partly open.

Lara stopped abruptly, her brow furrowing. "You don't think he keeps body parts in there, do you?"

"Why would you even think that?" Tristan couldn't quite keep the horror from his voice.

Lara turned and beamed a playful smile his way. Freshly scrubbed, her face looked clean and dewy, her skin begging to be touched. "I'm kidding. But I really don't know much about what vampires do in their spare time."

She slid her hand out of his and walked to the chest. Tristan focused on the elegant sway of her hips and the rivulet of water slipping from her hair to run down the length of her spine into the inviting crevice between her ass cheeks. Heat coiled in his groin, making his dick throb, swamping him with incredible need. "I think I've shown you a few times what we do for entertainment."

"Mmm…once or twice." She nudged the lid open all the way. "Oh my." She reached in and pulled out a pair of handcuffs, which she dangled from her index finger. "And I suppose when you get tired of playing big, bad, vampire, you play cop?"

Tristan groaned. Every masculine nerve in his body urged him to take what she was so playfully offering. But no matter how much he wanted to fuck her, he couldn't risk having her rush out of the mansion in broad daylight, the curse driving her where he couldn't follow.

If he allowed his brain to rule the rest of his overheated anatomy, he'd ask Hayden for another room before this went any further.

Yet being in the same room with Lara, sharing a bed, was the only way he could truly protect her. Or so Tristan told himself, though the excuse sounded feeble, even to him.

The silence between them sizzled with sexual tension and sizzling expectation. Knowing he'd lost the battle even before it started, he lunged, grabbed Lara around the waist and pinned her down on the bed, his body pressing down on hers, pushing her into the mattress. The handcuffs fell out of her hand.

"Is that what you want?" He growled. "A boring, donut-eating, *human* cop?"

His mouth hovered an inch from hers. He allowed his fangs to elongate and she rewarded him with a low, startled moan. Her eyes widened—but no longer in terror. Rather, hungry need and the smell of her arousal flooded Tristan's senses. Her nipples beaded against his chest.

"I want…" She licked her lips. The sight of the pink tip of her tongue made Tristan's cock twitch. "I want to feel you in me."

He shook his head. "You know I can't."

She squeaked a frustrated protest but her arms went up around his neck and her fingers threaded in his hair. "I don't want to talk about the curse. I don't even want to think about it." She watched him from beneath lowered lashes and shifted against his body so the heat of her cunt pressed against his thigh. She wriggled slightly, slicking his flesh with cream. "Just for tonight, let's pretend it doesn't exist."

Chapter Nine
ഔ

"Fuck me, Tristan," Lara whispered.

His body stiffened and he dug his fangs into his bottom lip. "Lara…" The word was a warning, low and guttural, as though torn right from his chest.

Lara shook her head. She slid her fingers through his long hair, loving the way the silky strands spilled over her skin and grazed her breast. "I don't want to hear protests or talk of the curse."

"If we don't stop it—"

She pressed her index finger against his lips. "I know. You and your brother have made the consequences very clear. If I'm going to die in three days, why would you deny me what I want the most?"

Tristan growled. "You are *not* going to die."

A nervous smile lifted her lips. "Yeah, well…there's always a chance we won't figure this out in time, isn't there?"

He slammed his mouth against hers hard, cutting off anything else she might have said. His tongue forced its way inside, leaving a moist trail over her swollen lips. She met him thrust for thrust, drawing him inside her mouth as he shifted and nudged his strong, muscular legs inside her spread thighs.

His potent arousal nudged her slick core. The intensity of the long, drawn-out kiss sent a shudder through her body, yet she couldn't banish the somber thoughts flashing through her mind.

Her pulse sped at the thought of her impending death. It still seemed so strange, like an obscure prediction that may or may not come true. If she'd heard it from a gypsy at a state fair, the morbid prognosis would be easy to deny. But she couldn't argue with the incoherence of primal fear that took hold when she gave in to Tristan.

Nor could she pretend that being with him wasn't a bad idea. A *very* bad idea.

It had been dangerous before, when she'd known him only as the saintly investor with a reputation for ruthlessness. He killed people who disobeyed him, for heaven's sake! Now that she knew the truth about his nature, she should be running for the door of her own volition, not writhing beneath him while practically begging for his cock.

She knew all these things. Logically, her brain prodded her in the direction of the door. He'd made it clear he wouldn't let her leave, but could he really hold her here against her will?

A chill of apprehension ran down her spine at the thought. Would he tie her to the bed if all else failed? And once he had her exactly where he wanted her, captive and willing, what would he do to her?

A low moan escaped her lips to disappear inside his mouth. Arousal slid along her skin, grazing a path that led straight to her pussy. Tristan's hard body pressed against hers everywhere, his erection blazing against her cunt even through the silky material of his boxers. She wanted him with a potent animal need that made her cunt muscles clench in anticipation.

She yearned to feel his length nestled in her heat, to welcome his body inside hers and forget about the curse for as long as his cock plunged into her. And if she had it her way, that would be all night.

He broke away at last, his ragged breathing matching hers. Cupping her face in his hands so she couldn't avoid his gaze, he narrowed his eyes, the swirling amber within giving him a dangerous, predatory look. "I won't let you run from me again, Lara."

She wiped moisture from his lower lip with her thumb. "Then either let me feel you—all of you—or let me go to my suite. Because what you're doing to me right now is cruel."

He lowered his head and nibbled at the nape of her neck. She held her breath, waiting for the sting of his fangs, her body tense against a pain that didn't come.

"I need you with me," he said, his voice hoarse and filled with a desperate desire that mirrored her own.

An idea formed in her mind, so simple it couldn't fail. "Then don't make me come," she whispered over the frantic pounding of her heart.

He moved faster than she could follow, grabbing both her wrists and pinning them into the mattress. He kneeled between her legs as he held her hands at her sides, his lips drawn into a thin line. "A few minutes ago, you were begging me to fuck you." His brows drew downward in a deep frown. "Is this about the guy you were with at the gallery? Are you eager to go back to him?"

She sighed in exasperation and rolled her eyes.

You fool. Why would you doubt what's happening between us? Why wouldn't you trust what my body is telling you?

"Not that it's any of your business…" she began, but stopped when she saw the sheepish grin spreading over his face.

"I'm sorry," he murmured, releasing her and bending his head to her breast. He circled a nipple with his tongue. "Forgive me."

She sucked in a breath, the sensations spreading through her body blending with the confusion slipping through her mind. Then suddenly, she understood.

"You read my mind." It wasn't a question.

"It's not intentional." He nipped at a tightly beaded nipple. "I can't control it, though I'm not sure I would even if I could."

141

She nibbled at her lower lip. Tingles ran over her skin as he fastened his mouth on her breast and sucked on her sensitive flesh. The knowledge that he could peer into her most intimate thoughts should have frightened her but it didn't. The idea that he was only a thought away if she needed him offered a deep, sensual sense of comfort.

Whenever she stopped to think about it long enough, she came to the same conclusion. Trusting him didn't make a whole lot of sense. Tristan was still just as controlling as he'd been all along, as adamant about knowing what she needed better than she did. Yet unlike her father's need to command her every move for the sake of proving his unquestionable authority, Tristan's dominion came from a deep-seated desire to keep her safe.

She understood that, and the knowledge both frightened and aroused her. In his arms, Lara felt protected, as though she'd stepped into her own private sanctuary.

She cleared her throat. "What I said earlier… I meant that you could fuck me without making me come."

Tristan's low chuckle vibrated through her skin. "You sure know how to make a guy feel good about himself."

"That's not what I meant and you know it." She swatted playfully at his shoulder then drew her hand back, fully aware that only an hour ago his flesh had been ripped apart by a silver bullet. Had he given his damaged body enough time to recover?

Tristan held his weight on his elbows and peered at her intently. "I'm okay now. My brothers are able to heal me better than anyone else."

She released a breath she didn't know she'd been holding. "I can tell you're very close. I envy that."

He slid his fingertips over her stomach and dipped them inside her dewy folds. "We've always been there for one another. I only wish Alexander had relocated to the United States along with Hayden and me."

She sighed with pleasure, her inner walls responding to his caress with quick throbbing spasms. She gritted her teeth. When she willed it, her self-control could rival anyone's and she fully planned to put it to the test tonight.

"I'd like to meet Alexander some day."

Tristan glanced at her, an unreadable emotion in his eyes. He nodded once briskly then returned his gaze to her pussy. His finger made slow, sensual circles around her clit, carefully avoiding the pleasure nub that could send a shattering orgasm streaming through her body before either of them could do anything to stop it.

Lara's heart clenched, instinctively grasping upon the thought that made him hesitate. She may not live long enough to meet his brother or anyone else for that matter. That realization was enough to cool her raging libido.

"I'm coming with you to see Illiana's brother."

Tristan shook his head. "You're not going anywhere. *I'll* go see him. You'll stay here, where it's safe."

Lara lifted herself on her elbows. "What makes you think you can order me around like a lap dog? I'm as involved in this as you are. Maybe more so since I don't see your life hanging by a thread."

Raw, untamed fury blazed in his eyes when he lifted his head to look at her. "There's an assassin out there. I won't allow you to put yourself in any more danger than you're already in."

"You won't *allow* me?" she asked between gritted teeth. "What makes you think you have any say in what I do?"

"This."

She didn't see him move but she didn't have to. His tongue scorched her already sensitive pussy as he licked a path down her slit. She trembled and fell back upon the mattress, bunching the sheets in both fists as her hips ground to the rhythm he set.

There would be no arguing with him. He made that clear with one word, though even that hadn't been necessary. The power he held over her should have sent her running away in terror but, God, his mouth clamped around her cunt felt too good, too *right*.

She thought she heard him chuckle against her pussy but she didn't stop to contemplate that. If he'd heard her thoughts, so be it. Her traitorous body responded to every flick of his tongue and she couldn't hide her reactions from him even if she wanted to.

He lay between her legs and she risked a peek at the top of his head as it moved to the rhythm of his mouth. She sighed with pleasure, feeling the intense, burning heat flare in her cunt and coil low in her belly, the waves of her climax ready to break within her if he so much as touched her clit.

Tristan grabbed her hips with both hands and pulled her closer. His tongue impaled her, a helpless prisoner of oral torture. She cried out, her fingers instinctively tangling in his hair. Her body shuddered with a violence that threatened to shatter her completely. She was so close…so close…

"Yes." The word broke from her throat, hoarse and filled with the same lust-induced frenzy that clouded her brain. She ached for the elusive orgasm, needing to come, aching for the shuddering pleasure of release.

"No."

He stopped a thought away from her ultimate release. The whimper that escaped her lips sounded unrecognizable to her own ears, a mixture of a whine and a soft mewling sound that couldn't possibly have come from her, yet somehow had.

In a flash of lucid thinking, she dragged her hand from his hair to her pussy, but Tristan was faster, grabbing her wrist and snapping the handcuff around it.

A moment later he'd secured the other end to the bedpost. He grabbed her left hand and held it beside the right while she struggled to break free, tears burning behind her eyelids.

"You pompous ass," she whispered. "I need this."

"Not coming was your idea, remember?"

She looked up at him, anger sending a wealth of wry retorts to settle on her tongue. One look in his eyes though, and they dissipated. She'd expected him to gloat, if not verbally, then at least inwardly. A hint of male arrogance should have lifted his lips in a smug smile. After all, what man who had just demonstrated his power over a woman's sexuality wouldn't lord it over her, especially when she was completely at his mercy?

Yet concern filled Tristan's gaze and his lips were drawn in a thin line. "I hate hurting you, even unintentionally." He released a deep breath then cupped her right breast in his palm, his thumb grazing her nipple. "I'm going to ask you this once and once only."

Lara narrowed her eyes in response, unsure where this was leading.

"Do you really want to climax, even knowing what will happen if you do?"

She swallowed hard and tilted her head, not quite willing to believe what she was hearing.

"Yes." Her whisper was barely more than a thought.

He nodded briskly, and with a speed she couldn't quite follow, released her breast and ripped his boxer shorts from his body, freeing his cock. Her mouth went dry when she glanced at his erection. The proud shaft jutted out from a mass of dark curls, eagerly spearing the air before it.

"Then so be it."

Tristan's gaze followed the play of emotions on Lara's face. Her dark eyes glistened, the luminous orbs shifting in their response from disbelief to admiration then to concern and ultimately to arousal when acceptance hit.

Her feelings flooded his senses, threatened to overwhelm him. Their bond had strengthened. He still couldn't tap into her thoughts whenever he wanted, but now her emotions were open to him. Had she chosen to share herself with him this way or was it yet another aspect of the curse neither of them could control?

"You are so beautiful," he told her, his fingertips brushing a fleeting touch against her cheek.

Lara bloomed under his compliment. Her cheeks heated, a rosy tint flooding her face. Even without the link, he'd have known exactly what she was feeling. She had the most wonderfully expressive features, open and completely honest. Even in the boardroom, surrounded by men who sought to rule her every move, she hadn't been able to hide her instinctual responses to the events unfolding around her.

In truth, Tristan thought she probably hadn't even tried. It wasn't in her to mask her emotions, to go through life with the cold and calculating outlook he'd had to adopt over the centuries.

Her tongue darted out between her lips for only a moment, leaving a trail of moisture in its wake. "Tristan," she whispered.

His name on her lips sent a searing awareness through his body. Her husky voice was more potent than any aphrodisiac, flooding his veins and swelling his already rock-hard cock even farther. Throbbing, pulsing need enveloped his balls. The pounding in his shaft deepened, bordering on pain.

She reached out with her free hand toward him and his soul answered. The deep longing in his chest startled him, as did the overwhelming sensation of needing to protect her. Naked and tied to the bed, she looked vulnerable and innocent, ready prey for anyone who wanted to hurt him.

"You're mine, Lara." The mattress dipped beneath his weight as he kneeled beside her.

She sighed. Her eyelids drifted closed in a slow, languid move and for a moment, he thought she'd argue. Then her clearly projected thought silenced his doubts.

Yours.

She met his eyes boldly, daring him to challenge what she felt. The depth of emotion swimming in her gaze was mirrored in his blood, the pounding of her heart matching the thrumming rhythm of his own eager desire.

"You don't need the handcuffs." She shook her wrist, the sound of metal slamming against metal resonating through the room with a series of rapid clangs.

He leaned over her until his mouth hovered a breath away from hers. "They're for your own protection."

"I've heard that before."

The remark stung, though he knew it shouldn't. It hadn't been meant for him. At least not directly. The moment he'd stepped into that boardroom, he'd realized what drove her. Her entire life had been about standing up to people who were supposed to love and protect her, and finding her own path without their support.

Resolve set a determined fire blazing in his blood. "I'm going to prove to you I'm nothing like the other men in your life." He ran his tongue along her lower lip and felt her tremble beneath him. "Nothing."

She sank back into the mattress and returned the playful swipe with her tongue. It grazed his, silky smooth and infinitely arousing, and he couldn't stop the groan that escaped his throat. "And just how do you plan to do that?"

"Slowly. Like this." His mouth strayed from hers. He placed small, wet kisses on her chin and along the soft skin of her throat.

Tristan. Oh God…

Her muscled tensed. The veins in her neck corded as she clenched her teeth, expecting him to take what he wanted right then and there.

His fangs answered the sensual call of her blood roaring just beneath the surface of her satiny skin, a mere nip away from gushing into his mouth. He ignored it.

He kissed a path down her breastbone and down to the hollow between her breasts. She tasted like sweat and arousal and *Lara*, a heady combination that was hers alone.

She relaxed, a breath of air escaping her lips as his fangs moved away from her throat.

His dick swelled painfully, roaring its displeasure at being made to wait. The hunger urged him on. The animalistic, primal part of his nature cried out for her, begging her to sate the craving as only she could.

A rough, determined ache of powerful need coiled low in Tristan's stomach. His teeth dug into his lower lip and he allowed himself one small indulgence by nipping at a tightly puckered nipple. Lara gasped at the unexpected sensation, but didn't thrash against the mattress or use her free hand to fight him off.

Instead, she arched her back and pushed her chest forward, closer to his mouth. He could smell her fear. It was genuine this time, not caused by some magical affliction she couldn't control. The scent of it mixed with her arousal, unmistakably feminine, infinitely maddening.

When she spoke, her voice was surprisingly steady and silkily seductive. "I'm yours. Take what you need."

A drop of blood sprang to the surface of her skin, its beaded crimson staining the dewy flesh of her nipple. He laved the tender spot with his tongue, closing the wound. His head swam in a fog of lust and desperation.

"Do you understand what you're saying?" The words were ripped from his throat in a frenzy of hopeful agony.

She couldn't possibly realize the depth of the gift she offered him, yet somehow, she did. He felt it all through their bond—her apprehension, her complete trust, her utter certainty that she was doing the right thing.

She held nothing back. Her thoughts tumbled inside her mind. She was eager to share herself with him in every way, to give him the one thing his immortal nature craved beyond all else.

The gift she offered him freely made his head spin. For centuries, he'd known he could only feed on one condition—the woman whose essence he tasted had to be in the throes of orgasm. That knowledge was as real to him as the knowledge that the Earth's gravity held him upright or that he couldn't step into daylight without perishing under the bright rays of the sun.

Without that rampant pleasure clouding his victim's senses, she'd scream in horror as soon as he sank his fangs into her flesh. Her terror would overwhelm her. She'd not only peg him as an unnatural creature but as a violent criminal.

As a result, vampires were forced to silence their victims once they started to scream, sometimes permanently. That wasn't the existence Tristan wanted.

He had no qualms about taking a life when the situation called for it, but he couldn't come to terms with the fact that someone would need to die in order for him to feed. Donors were the only other option but he'd never wanted the attachment such a relationship would bring.

But Lara had nothing to gain from offering herself to him.

"You won't hurt me," she said, though whether to him or to reassure herself, Tristan didn't know.

The dark part of his soul whispered eager encouragement. Tristan slipped his palm over her breast, feeling the weight of the soft mound in his hand. She slipped her fingers between them, grabbing his aching cock and stroking it with a velvet-smooth touch.

Tristan's fangs found their mark. He dove his teeth deep into her flesh. Her grip on his shaft tightened, her fist enclosing him like a vise. The sweet pain she inflicted was nothing compared to the hurt she must have felt, but she endured the sting without so much as a muffled cry of protest.

Tristan closed his eyes, lost in the ambrosial taste of her blood. Her essence flowed into his veins, leaving a trail of swirling heat in its wake that led straight to his groin.

Perhaps, he thought as his cock throbbed in her hand and her taste flooded his tongue, she also had nothing to lose. She knew about the curse and her inescapable fate. She knew about his nature and his need for her blood.

And she'd accepted both.

Unable to tear his mouth away from her breast, Tristan continued drinking long after he should have stopped. Lara arched into him, slid her heels up against her ass and spread her legs as her hips left the mattress. And still, she made no sound.

At last he pulled away, delirious, her flavor flooding his senses. Blood flowed freely from the twin puncture wounds on either side of her nipple, dripping down her creamy white skin. He lapped at the stream and sucked her nipple into his mouth, letting the healing properties of his saliva close the lesions.

Her chest heaved beneath him and her breath came in soft, strangled gasps. Guilt washed over Tristan, settling like lead in the pit of his stomach.

He'd been selfish. She'd shared every part of herself with him willingly and he'd done nothing for her in return.

"Thank you," he whispered, sliding his tongue in the tender valley between her breasts.

His hand slid down her belly to cup her mound. Cream clung to his skin, warm and inviting. He delved two fingers between her folds and she spread her legs, thrusting her hips upward in arching eagerness to meet his hand.

"I saw the woman on the balcony." Lara's husky tone jolted his cock to pulsing awareness. It throbbed in her firm grip.

He shifted so he could lick a path down her stomach while remaining kneeling at her side. He wanted her to hold his cock forever or at least until he could bury it to the hilt inside her moist, eager pussy.

His head between her legs, one hand playing within the dewy wetness slicking her labia, Tristan lapped a slow, sensual circle around her clit. "What woman?"

"The one you and your brother were with last night at the art gallery."

Tristan's heart skipped a beat at the raw tilt of her voice. He felt her jealousy as though it were his own. The need to reassure her, to explain that Illiana had meant nothing to him settled heavy on his tongue.

Before he could say anything though, she continued. "I wanted to feel what she felt in your arms. You should have seen the look on her face when you two pleasured her…drank from her. Oh!" Tristan shoved two fingers inside Lara's tight channel and she bucked against his hand.

"Don't try to distract me," she admonished, but he heard the playful lilt behind the severe words.

She slicked her palm over the tip of his cock, spreading the dripping bead of pre-cum down his shaft with enticingly fluid movements.

"Okay." He sucked her plump labia into his mouth then released it. "I won't."

"I mean it, Tristan." Lara squirmed as he thrust his fingers rhythmically inside her. She shifted her grip on his cock, lowering her hand to cup his balls. "I want you to do to me what you did to her."

He licked a path down her slit, past his fingers and the tempting entrance to her channel. Lara lifted her ass, giving him greater access to every delicious inch of her.

He raised his head from her depths for only a moment. "No."

She squeezed his balls in her palm, the delicious agony sending a rush of heat to settle in his cock. More pre-cum oozed from the slit at the tip, slicking his shaft. "Would you care to reconsider that answer?"

Tristan gritted his teeth. Gently, he freed himself from her hold and straightened then moved to kneel between her parted thighs. He grabbed her calves and lifted her legs, positioning her ankles on his shoulders. She moaned then bit her lip to stifle it. The look she gave him dripped with satisfaction.

"No," he repeated, slicking his fingers with her cream. Her dark eyes narrowed and she shook her head.

I should have known you'd never let me get the upper hand. Not even for a moment.

He grinned, the tips of his fangs scraping against his lower lip. "I don't just want to do to you what I did to her. I want to do more to you. So much more."

Tristan reached around her leg and parted her ass cheeks. He used his index finger to circle the puckered rosebud of her anus. She moaned her understanding and watched him with barely contained lust as he circled the tight hole with his fingertip.

"This is what I did to Illiana."

He thrust inside Lara gently, waiting for her ass to adjust to the intrusion then pushed deeper and deeper still until her muscles clenched, pulling his finger in past the knuckle.

"Oh." Lara sighed and made small circles with her hips. "That feels incredible."

"But that's *all* I did to her. With her."

He closed the rest of the space between them and positioned the tip of his cock at the entrance to her pussy. Her pink, velvet-soft labia quivered with the same anticipation pouring through his veins.

And then the dam that held his self-control in check broke inside him and he slammed into her welcoming heat. Lara keened her pleasure and met his thrust with a rhythm of her own. His finger moved inside her anus, making her cunt slam against the base of his shaft with each upward motion.

Her pussy sheathed him completely, wrapping around him, tightening and gripping his cock in its fiery clasp.

"Come," she urged as she bucked against his hand, impaling her sweet cunt completely on his aching cock. "Come with me."

He couldn't fight her. Just the slick, sliding motion of his shaft delving deep inside her was sheer torture. Sensations streamed through his body, clenching his muscles, driving him over the edge.

This time, he didn't have to feed. He could watch Lara's eyes as her climax tightened her inner walls. Her pussy spasmed and she cried out, holding his gaze, taking him over the edge with her.

Streams of pleasure roared through his body. He spilled his seed in gushing spurts, soaking her womb. Lara clung to him with her legs, her thighs, her free hand gripping his arm and her fingernails digging into his skin.

Her ecstasy slammed into him, merging with his own. She held his gaze boldly, her lips forming a perfect O as her cries resonated through the room.

I'm not afraid of you. I'm not afraid of you. I'm not afraid of you.

She repeated the thought like a mantra, each word ringing out clearly in Tristan's mind as she braced herself against the effects of the curse. Her lips tilted upward in a smile and for a moment, he allowed himself to hope she'd overcome the inevitable magic effects that had doomed his bloodline for generations.

Then horror widened her eyes and every last shred of his optimism faded.

She cried out, but this time the scream was animalistic, instinctual. It echoed with unbridled agony. She slammed her closed fist against his chest, tears streaming down her cheeks. Wild, primal fear distorted her soft features. Her lips, only moments ago parted in sensual delight, now pressed together as she fought to stifle another scream.

He caught her slender wrist as she aimed a second flailing punch at his chest. His cock slid out of her pussy with a loud pop, releasing a stream of cum down her inner thigh.

He let go of her arm for only a moment while he moved as fast as thought, pulled out a second pair of handcuffs from Hayden's chest and returned to secure her free wrist to the bedpost. Betrayal and terror shone in her dark eyes. He tried to look beneath the fear, to tap in to their sensual connection and call out to the part of her soul that hadn't been affected by the curse, but she fought his efforts by thrashing against her bonds.

She looked beautiful, like an ethereal captive creature with her wild silky curls, wide eyes and tear-streaked cheeks.

For the first time in centuries, Tristan felt his heart break. The wall he'd erected to protect himself since his wife's death shattered as he watched Lara fight to free herself, wild with fear at the sight of him.

Tristan leaned down and pressed a cheek to her sweat-slicked forehead. She cried out at the contact and he quickly pulled back, grimacing. "Sleep well, baby."

A soul-shattering wail was the only response she could give. The metal clang of the handcuffs being yanked against the bedpost resounded like a death knell behind him. Willing himself not to look back, he left the room and slammed the heavy door behind him.

Chapter Ten

જી

A sweet, wet, infinitely tender kiss swept over Lara's lips. She moaned and parted them, welcoming the gentle intrusion of a tongue sliding inside her mouth.

Firm hands cupped her face, tilted her chin. The kiss deepened, bringing with it a pulsing wave of heat to her pussy. She didn't fight the sensation but gave herself over to it, drinking in the taste of mint and tangy metallic copper.

Her body hurt all over, a delicious pounding ache that started between her thighs and swept through her limbs. It focused in the swelling between her legs that let her know she'd been thoroughly and completely fucked.

She moaned against the mouth that stole her breath, her tongue lingering on the sensual flavor assaulting her taste buds. Her pussy heated, moisture flooded her core. She tried to bring her legs together but an inexplicable weight prevented her from moving as she should.

She blinked her eyes open to the sights and sounds surrounding her. Her breath caught in her throat as Tristan filled her field of vision, his amber-flecked green eyes boring into hers. Around them, laughter and gregarious chatter echoed loudly through the cavernous room. A hard surface pressed against her back and she didn't have to look down to know that food covered her body.

Ever since her first night on display at Bitter Sweet, she'd thought of the place as her own private haven. A wicked, decadent haven, sure, but a haven nevertheless. Her father would never find her there. She could bare herself to strangers without worrying about her family name or what the great Senior Montgomery would think if he saw her this way.

155

Here, even with strangers' hands lingering too long on her skin when they picked up a delicious morsel, she felt safe. Their admiration warmed her, aroused her. Their approval slid inside hidden corners of her heart, temporarily filling a need she thought would never be genuinely satiated.

Until Tristan came along.

He pulled away as if sensing her thoughts. She grinned up at him, letting all the happiness filling her heart pool into her mind and flow outward to him. He could read her thoughts when they were strong enough so she concentrated on escalating the slew of emotions and projecting them outside herself.

The laughter died down. Silence enveloped the room, thick with anticipation. She glanced behind Tristan and noticed the crowd had formed a circle around them.

"Don't be frightened," Tristan said. He slid his elegant suit jacket off his shoulders to reveal a crisp white shirt that outlined lean muscles. She licked her lips, yearning to run her tongue over the dips and valleys of the planes of his chest then lower, over his hard abs, and lower still to circle the base of his hot, pulsing cock.

"I'm not," she said, meaning it. She wasn't afraid of him or of the men who watched her with hungry, lust-filled gazes.

He nodded approvingly. One hand slid to his zipper and drew it down. His pants pooled around his ankles. He shed his shoes and socks then stepped out of the pants slowly. Tonight he hadn't worn boxers. His cock thrust out, swollen and tempting, jutting out from a mass of short, black curls.

"If I asked you to fuck someone else," Tristan asked, unbuttoning his shirt, "would you do it while I watched?"

A collage of conflicting emotions scattered through Lara. She wanted to open her mouth to say no, but a wave of arousal shredded the thought. Her nipples beaded and her breasts felt swollen and full, needing to be touched, fondled.

Tristan took a step closer then another, his cock drifting toward her. He waved his hand in her direction and the food weighing her down disappeared, leaving her completely naked. She swallowed back a protest, resisting the urge to cover her mound with her hand. She was used to being nude in public but the food had offered some protection from covetous stares.

Tristan stopped close enough to her table that if she reached out with her tongue, she could to taste the bead of wetness glistening at the tip of his cock.

Her pussy throbbed. A barrage of images flooded her thoughts. In her mind, she saw herself being fucked. Thoroughly.

Tristan's cock would fill her mouth while another man would slam hard between her legs, thrusting inside her pussy. Then they'd pull her off the table and bend her over it, spreading her thighs apart from behind.

Tristan would part her ass cheeks and impale her tightly puckered hole while another man would kneel in front of her, his fingers delving inside her cunt while he tongued her clit. The onslaught of sensations would surge through her body, making her come in wave after wave of delicious, heart-pounding, maddening orgasms.

Moisture pooled between her legs and dripped onto the table. Tristan nudged her lips with his cock. "Suck me off while you think about it, beautiful."

She opened to him and took his shaft in her mouth as far as she was able, letting the heavy weight settle on her tongue. Funny, she thought as she closed her eyes and devoured the musky taste of him, how after a lifetime of struggling against men who sought to control every move she made, it was so damn easy to submit to one.

Tristan's fingers gripped her hair and he held her head close while he fucked her mouth, thrusting the length of his thick cock between her lips. She moaned around the intrusion, the pulsing in her cunt intensifying with every sweep of her tongue over the tip of his cock. Liquid, musky and coppery, like the flavor she'd come to associate with him, filled her mouth, drowning her senses in the heady aroma.

Something wet touched her pussy. She squirmed and opened her eyes but Tristan's grip was firm, allowing her head little movement. She couldn't see anything but him, the coarse black curls brushing her nose with each plunge of his cock inside her mouth.

The pressure between her legs intensified. She gasped as she recognized the feel of a slick tongue sliding inside her folds, prodding the entrance to her channel. Someone's face pressed against her cunt as the tongue worked its magic, sweeping down her slit then back up to circle her clit and nudge it gently.

Lara shuddered, knowing it wouldn't take much of the delicious assault to make her come. Tristan's muscles stiffened and his cock swelled farther, growing impossibly hard inside her mouth.

The exquisite rapture streaming through her cunt ended unexpectedly. The sudden loss of the incredible caress made her shiver. Her lower lips were soaked with her juices and saliva. A cold stream of breath flowed over her wet skin, a delicious contrast to the burning, needy ache gathered at the apex of her thighs.

Then a sharp stab of pleasure-pain pierced her upper inner thigh and the world came crashing down around her.

At once her pussy responded to the extra stimulation by releasing a steady stream of shudders through her body. Her muscles clenched and wetness soaked her thighs as the orgasm hit its peak, making every nerve ending in her body tremble with agonizing pleasure.

Simultaneously, Tristan released his hot, salty seed inside her mouth. It flowed down her throat almost faster than she could swallow it. She felt him shudder as he came, his body undergoing the same ecstatic agony as her own.

And then within the span of a breath, terror took hold. It slammed into her, dissipating the remnants of her orgasm with a force she couldn't have anticipated. It knocked the air out of her lungs and sent her sprawling backward on the table.

She glanced wildly at the faces gathered around her. Where a minute ago there had been men now stood monsters, their misshapen faces twisted into vicious scowls. They advanced upon her, arms outstretched, claws aiming for her bare skin.

She opened her mouth to scream but no sound came out. Between her legs, a familiar face stared back at her, his eyes kind even as blood dripped off his lips.

Her blood.

Her insides gave a hollow lurch and terrifying agony spread like wildfire through her veins. She recognized him, the man who'd bitten her.

"Hayden." Her mouth moved to form the word but nothing happened. Her voice had vanished along with any semblance of normalcy.

Frantic, Lara dove off the table. She stumbled and caught herself before she fell, instinctively knowing that if the beasts touched her, death would follow, and it wouldn't be swift or merciful.

"Enough!"

The deep, masculine voice echoed through the room, silencing the eager moans of the creatures huddled around her. She'd heard that word before, spoken in that same manner, but she couldn't focus enough to bring it to the forefront of her mind.

Lara shook her head. It hurt too much to think clearly.

She looked up into a pair of amber-flecked eyes and for a moment her breath caught in her throat. A dark slash of black eyebrows pulled down in concern. The man's long black hair hung loose around his shoulders, framing a chiseled jaw, wide cheekbones and a straight nose. Fangs, sharp and menacing, slid out from beneath his upper lip.

He reached up with a speed that surprised her, though she knew it shouldn't have.

A scream caught in her throat. She flinched and took a step back—right into a solid wall. He had her cornered and she knew it. Worse yet, judging by the way his eyes narrowed as he stepped closer, he knew it too.

Dizziness swept over Lara. Hot tears clogged her throat. "Let me go."

Her plea went unanswered.

The man reached up and cupped her neck in his broad hand. He tilted her head and lowered his mouth to the pulsing vein in her throat. "Mine," he said, the word sliding over her skin like a lover's caress.

Lara shrieked. The sound boomed against the walls of the lounge as though amplified, startling them both. Tristan lifted his head, blood dripping off his chin.

"Tristan." She said his name softly, tentatively, a mere whisper barely penetrating a fog of uncertainty.

The dream disintegrated into a puff of smoke but not before she saw his lips curve upward in a smile.

* * * * *

Lara blinked her eyes open. Her heart pounded and her pussy leaked another drop of cream as she shifted on the silky soft sheets.

Her arms hurt. "Oh God," she murmured, remembering the handcuffs slamming around her wrists.

She lifted herself into a sitting position, surprised when her hands fell forward to settle in her lap. Her breath came in harsh, ragged gasps. She leaned her head back and rubbed at her sore wrists. Most of the candles that had burned so brightly when she and Tristan had entered the room now sat in darkness. A few still sputtered, smoke trailing upward from the rapidly dwindling flames. Shadows enveloped the room, mimicking the dimness of twilight.

Lara scrubbed a palm over her face in an attempt to banish the last trailing remnants of the nightmare. It had all felt so real. She could still taste the heavy weight of Tristan's cock on her tongue, could still feel the tongue sweeping over her pussy.

Hayden's tongue. Hayden's mouth.

Lara trembled as she remembered the intense orgasm he'd caused her. An answering pulsing heat flooded her cunt and she released a deep breath she hadn't realized she'd been holding.

From the moment she'd laid eyes on Tristan, her world had been turned upside down. She needed to get out of here. The curse was still out there, haunting her, terrorizing her even while she slept.

She had to find a way to end the threat. Then and only then, could she truly deal with her feelings for Tristan.

With one last shuddering breath, Lara slid from the bed. Her feet sank into the plush carpet. The air in the room was warm, comfortable, and it caressed her sweat-slicked skin, drying it.

In three long strides, she'd crossed the distance to the door. She molded her palm around the handle and pulled.

Nothing happened.

She tried again and again, to no avail. In frustration, she slammed her hand against the wooden frame. The hard slap echoed through the room. She cried out, calling first Tristan's name then, when that received no response, Hayden's. She alternated both until her throat ached. Each time, her voice bounced back at her, taunting her with its high-pitched whine.

Lara let out an angry growl. She should have known. She should have fucking known Tristan would be true to his word. He wouldn't let her leave. At least, not without him.

Once again, Tristan Chance had the upper hand.

And there wasn't a damn thing she could do about it.

Chapter Eleven

ဢ

"Why aren't you back yet?" Marie asked. She'd offered no other greeting after picking up the phone.

Tristan leaned back in a rickety chair. One of its legs was shorter than the other three and it wobbled unsteadily beneath his weight. A dim haze of cigarette smoke surrounded him, making it hard to see past the scarred wooden table in front of him. "I haven't yet found what I'm looking for."

"Then hurry up, boss. I've spent the past couple of nights doing damage control and I think I've just about managed to convince everyone who matters that the picture in the paper was a staged publicity stunt."

"A publicity stunt," he repeated, scrubbing a palm over his face. "When was the last time you saw Tom Cruise's cock hang out of his pants while he almost got hit by a truck in the middle of the night?"

"Wasn't that a scene in the latest *Mission Impossible* movie?"

Tristan groaned. "If it was, I hope he got hazard pay."

Marie ignored the last comment. "Anyway, it looks like it worked. I've got appointments lined up for you every night for three weeks and these aren't the kind of people who are willing to wait for your vacation to end."

"Good. Tell them I'll be in New York in four days."

"Not good enough. I need you here tomorrow to meet with Luciano and his boys."

Tristan let out a low whistle. "I've been after Luciano for years. How did you finally convince the head of the biggest New York crime family to meet with me?"

He could almost hear her smile through the phone and knew she was beaming. "I've got skills you know nothing about, boss."

Tristan groaned. "I don't *want* to know about them."

Marie's warm chuckle made him miss New York. "I'll spare you the nitty-gritty. But it seems there's something he needs. Something you have."

"Money."

"Bingo. Makes the world go 'round, boss."

"Money doesn't solve all problems."

Marie sucked in a breath between her teeth. "Who are you and what have you done with Tristan Chance?"

Thunder rolled in the distance, insistent and foreboding. A chill ran up Tristan's spine.

He rubbed the bridge of his nose and inhaled the scents of sweat, smoke and cheap beer permeating the air of the cluttered bar. The neon sign outside proclaimed it to be Hell's Own, and judging by the stench, the peanut shells littering the floor and the state of the ragged clientele, he was inclined to believe it.

"Tomorrow's impossible. Reschedule with Luciano."

She tsked her displeasure but eventually relented. "Sunday night then. You're sure you'll be here?"

Tristan sank his teeth into his lower lip. The memory of Lara's panic-stricken face was imprinted on his mind, taunting him each time he blinked. She'd looked so horrified after they'd made love, as though she'd just been fucked by the Devil himself.

Perhaps she had been, he mused, remembering the smell of her skin, the feel of her soft breast beneath his palm. He had to save her. Not doing so wasn't an option.

"I'm sure."

A young man dressed in jeans and a black T-shirt walked past Tristan and headed for the small stage at the corner of the bar. He held a guitar case in one hand. "Marie, I gotta go. My appointment's shown up."

"You're doing business while you're away? I thought this trip was purely for pleasure."

He grimaced. "A little of both, I suppose."

He could tell she wanted to press him for details but didn't. He was grateful for that. "Okay. If you're not here Sunday night, you'll answer to me."

Tristan laughed, picturing his five-feet-three assistant, fists perched on hips, nose scrunched up in displeasure. "I'd rather take my chances with Luciano."

"That's what I thought. Luciano may reschedule but I'm not nearly as forgiving."

He was still smiling when he slid his phone into his pocket. Since the day he'd used his IOU to purchase her services, Marie had brought a spark into his business that had been sorely lacking. She was an indentured servant, unable to leave his side for as long as she lived, but she never acted as though that was an imposition—simply a fact of life. As soon as she began working for him, Tristan found he was excited to come in to work in the evening, knowing his contracts would be in order, his appointments lined up for the night, his clients well taken care of.

He knew he'd never approach his personal life with the same enthusiasm but that was fine. Work kept him busy. There would always be people in need of the services he offered. He had no reason to take a night off, and the only indulgences he'd allowed himself only lasted as long as it took him to feed.

Until he met Lara.

A bright flood of white light spilled over the man on stage, cutting through the dark haze of smoke. It illuminated his features and Tristan guessed he had to be in his early thirties. He wore his short brown hair swept back from his wide forehead. The unkempt strands didn't appear slicked down with hair product but simply the result of brushing his fingers through them one too many times. His lean face and aquiline nose suited the brooding young artist look. A dark goatee bracketed his thin lips.

Julian Smith wasn't exactly what Tristan had expected but then again, he hadn't expected to find the man in a place like this either.

The sounds of boisterous laughter drowned out Julian's voice as he began to sing. The patrons, ranging from bikers dressed in heavy leather jackets and large chains to men in plaid shirts clutching desperately at stubs of cigarettes, didn't even pause to glance at Julian.

A hint of empathy ran through Tristan. He remembered what it was like to be ignored, to not be taken seriously when all he'd wanted to do was prove himself to the world. He saw the same look in Julian's eyes as he'd seen in Lara's in the Montgomery Suites boardroom when her father wouldn't even cast a glance her way.

The love song Julian crooned was an old one. The words spoke of longing, of unfulfilled desire and trembling, desperate hope. It reminded Tristan of simpler days, before the world began to move faster and faster, before technology made simple face-to-face meetings a thing of the past.

Julian's voice streamed through the room, confident and powerful. Though the man's eyes looked haunted and uneasy, his tone didn't waver. The song ended on a perfect note, one the patrons of Hell's Own barely heard.

Julian sighed. He cast a glance around the room and his shoulders slumped visibly. Then he cleared his throat and jutted out his chin before beginning another song.

Tristan rose and made his way to the stage, elbowing a man out of his way in the process. He heard the sharp string of profanity tossed his way, gauged the challenge and venom in the voice behind it then decided the threat wasn't important enough to merit the wasted time. Julian was the only link he had to the curse and time had been running out since the first day he'd met Lara.

He stepped on stage and grabbed Julian's arm, startling him in mid-song. "We need to talk."

Julian turned tired eyes on Tristan and covered the mike with his hand to keep his voice from booming through the bar. Not that the patrons seemed to care the entertainment had stopped. "Hey, man, I've got another half an hour before my break."

Outside, thunder rumbled ominously, the sound almost indistinguishable from Tristan's growl. He tightened his grip until his knuckles turned white. "Now."

Julian grimaced. "Fine. If I get fired though, it's on your head."

Tristan shrugged. "I can live with that."

With only a few days left before the curse's deadline, Tristan didn't much care whether the man lost his job. Lara would lose much more than that if he didn't find a way to track down someone who knew enough about the magic to put a stop to it. Permanently.

"Where to?" Julian asked as they stepped off the stage.

Tristan glanced at the crowded bar and jerked a thumb over his shoulder toward the fire escape. "That way."

They pushed through the thick metal door and took the stairs down toward the back entrance. The exit opened onto a dark alley. The smell of stale sewer water and rotting garbage clogged Tristan's throat. Still, he found he preferred it to the stench of humanity inside the bar.

Lightning flashed across the sky, cracking a white line down the middle of the inky velvet. The scent of the impending storm cut through the cloying aromas in the alley. Humidity hung heavy in the atmosphere, making Tristan's linen suit stick to his skin.

Julian pulled out a pack of cigarettes and stuck one between his thin lips. "What was so important that you dragged me off the stage in the middle of my set?" he asked around the cigarette, the words slightly slurred.

"I need a history lesson. How much do you know about your past?"

Julian narrowed his eyes. "You've got to be fucking kidding me. You want…what, exactly? My family history? My medical records? What?"

"I'm looking for information on Katherine Smith."

Julian shook his head. "Like I told the other guy who came asking, I don't know any Katherine." He inhaled deeply then coughed, his thin shoulders shaking with the effort.

"My brother told me you two had spoken but I wanted to meet with you myself. I didn't expect you to know her personally. She lived about six hundred years ago, somewhere in London."

Julian blew a thin stream of blue smoke into the air. "Look, man, I'm not into genealogy. My sister and I were born in Florida. We lived with my mother until we were old enough to move out. Then we struck out on our own, more or less. My grandparents both died when I was six. That's all I know."

Disappointment rippled in Tristan's stomach. He forced himself to take a deep breath and try another tactic. "Is there a history of the occult in your family? Do you practice magic?"

Julian snorted. "I've never been any good at those sleight-of-hand gags kids fooled around with."

"That's not the kind of magic I'm talking about." Tristan crossed his arms over his chest and peered intently into Julian's eyes, trying to gauge whether the man held back information, perhaps to protect his family. The only thing he saw in Julian's gaze was utter exhaustion and deep-seated sadness.

"You think if I could do any of that voodoo shit I'd be in this hellhole?" Julian chuckled at his unintentional pun, but the smile disappeared a moment later. His lips pulled down into a frown. "My mother talked about superstition as though it were real. Giving someone the evil eye, that sort of thing. I never paid much attention though."

Tristan failed to keep the chagrin from his voice. "Do you have any other siblings in the city? Cousins? Any relatives at all who might know something about Katherine Smith and the type of magic she was involved in six hundred years ago?"

Julian's forehead creased. He leaned over the metal railing and took another deep puff of his cigarette. "Nope," he said at last, shaking his head. "There's no one else."

The agony of his impotence slammed into Tristan like a punch to the gut. Hayden had spent a small fortune talking to every occultist he could find. None of them had heard of a curse like the one he described. They'd prescribed herbs, spells chanted at midnight on a full-moon night, crystal cures...nothing had worked.

Tristan now believed that finding someone familiar with Katherine's unique brand of magic was key. But the chances of finding such a person six hundred years after the woman's death when he only had a few days in which to do it seemed unlikely at best, impossible at worst.

Like his brother, he'd be forced to watch the woman he loved perish before his eyes. Even if he kept Lara locked up somewhere for the next few days as he was doing now, he knew the curse would find her. Hayden had explained that once time ran out, death was a simple matter of her heartbeat coming to a stop for no physically explainable reason.

He couldn't let that happen. He *wouldn't.*

But the answers didn't lie with Julian Smith. The man had enough trouble of his own.

The metal door slammed against the wall. A small man with spiky hair and a beer belly that hung low over his belt threw a backpack at Julian and tossed the black guitar case at his feet. Tristan caught the backpack with lightning-fast reflexes before it found its mark.

"I don't pay you to take smoke breaks in the middle of your shift." He spat on Julian's shoes. "In fact, as of tonight, I don't pay you at all."

The man spun around and dashed inside a moment before the skies opened. The rain fell in steady waves, pelting Tristan and Julian with cold beads of water that made their hair and clothes stick to their skin.

Julian tossed his cigarette over the railing. He bent down to pick up the guitar case then slung the backpack Tristan handed him over his shoulder. Bending his head against the torrential downpour, he descended the few steps to the sidewalk. Hesitating, he turned toward Tristan. "I'm sorry I couldn't help you find what you were looking for," he said, raising his voice to be heard above the storm. "It looks like neither one of us is having a particularly good night." He offered a small wave then ambled down the street, shoulders hunched against the rain.

Pity jolted Tristan's feet. He fell into step beside Julian, taking in the man's soaked clothes, his shaggy hair, the deep disillusionment in his eyes. He reached out and gripped his arm again, stopping him in mid-stride.

Julian eyed him warily. "What now? I told you I don't—"

"Have you ever been to New York?"

Julian nodded. "Once, on a high-school field trip." His brows furrowed. "Why?"

Tristan reached inside the front pocket of his suit jacket and pulled out his wallet. It didn't take him long to locate the business card he sought. In moments, the rain soaked through the cardstock and left it hanging limply in his hand but the brightly colored text showed clearly against the soggy paper.

"Go see Dick at Bitter Sweet." He tapped his fingernail against the card. "It's on the corner of Fifth and Broadway. Tell him you're applying for the newly vacated solo singer position."

Julian looked dubious. "And he'll hire me, just like that?"

"He will if you tell him Tristan Chance sent you."

The ink wasn't even dry on their contract yet and Richard probably still trembled at the thought of Tristan's return. This would do absolutely nothing for Tristan's reputation as a ruthless force to be reckoned with. Marie would have to do some serious damage control when he returned and she wasn't going to be happy about it. Tristan sighed and pressed the card into Julian's palm. "Tell him I'm calling in a favor."

He was halfway across the street when he heard Julian's shout over the roar of another peal of thunder. He slid his hands into his pockets and turned around.

Julian hurried to catch up to him. "I don't know if this is going to mean anything to you but I have a great-aunt who lives on the outskirts of London. I wouldn't even have thought of it but I remembered her when you gave me the card."

An anxious heat pooled low in Tristan's stomach. "Go on."

"I only met her once when I was five but I recall the way she held me before we left. She looked right into my eyes and said, 'All things in life are bittersweet, but none so much as love'. Sappy, huh?"

"Yeah," Tristan agreed, not trusting himself to say anything else. "Sappy."

"She's not a true Smith though, so it probably won't matter. Anyway, her name is Annabelle Doherty and she's absolutely ancient. I mean, she was old even when I was little. She runs a local herb shop in Midwich. The locals say she dabbles in love potions and the like. Personally, our family always thought she was…" He made a circle with his index finger around his temple. "Nuts. But hey, it's cheaper to let her wander around the village then to put her into a home. And it's not like she's hurt anyone or anything."

A thrill pounded through Tristan's body. He grabbed Julian's shoulders and squeezed, hope building in his chest. "Thank you."

Julian's grimaced and pulled away from Tristan's iron grip. "No worries, man. Hope you find what you're looking for."

Oh he would, Tristan vowed silently as he broke into a supernatural run toward Hayden's mansion.

Lara's life depended on it.

* * * * *

Lara closed her eyes and tried to even her breathing as she heard the catch on the lock click open. She hadn't dared sleep since the nightmare but there hadn't been much else to do in the small, enclosed space. She'd thought about perusing the chest at the foot of the bed again but the idea of pleasuring herself without Tristan held no appeal...a fact that had only served to anger her further.

It wasn't fair. Why should Tristan have any power over her orgasms? It was bad enough that every time she had one around him she went wild with fear. She should have been delighted he'd left her alone long enough to indulge in a much-needed release with no side effects.

The door closed. Tristan's footsteps fell softly on the plush carpet as he neared the bed.

Lara kept her eyes tightly shut. A slew of thoughts ran through her mind, each suggesting a more vicious form of attack than the last. Tristan couldn't keep her here against her will. That was kidnapping and as far as she knew, it was still illegal. Laws applied to vampires as much as they applied to humans...didn't they?

The wait for him to reach her side seemed interminable. When at long last Tristan's breath caressed her cheek, instinctively Lara held hers.

"I know you're not sleeping. I can feel the turmoil warring within you." He lowered his voice to a mischievous whisper. "And even if I didn't...your fists are clenched."

172

For a brief moment, she thought about lifting that clenched fist and making contact with his jaw. The image was absurdly satisfying.

Tristan laughed—a deep, rich laughter that set her blood on fire. "You wouldn't be the first woman to take a swing at me."

Lara blinked her eyelids open, intending to tell Tristan exactly what she thought of him and his arrogant, inexcusable behavior...and met his amber-flecked green gaze. It was all she could do to stifle an unbidden groan. Dressed in the sharp, beautifully cut charcoal suit she'd come to expect, the man oozed raw animal sex appeal from every pore. It dripped from him in heavy waves, tempting her to slide her hands beneath the suit jacket, to taste the silky softness of his lips.

Lara pulled the top sheet higher up her body and rose to a sitting position to lean against the headrest. Only one candle still remained lit on the dresser closest to the bed, its flickering light casting myriad dancing shadows over Tristan's shadowy profile.

She eyed him with the frostiest glare she could manage while every nerve ending in her body pulsed with trembling need. It would be so easy to let the sheet fall, reach out and pull him to her for that tantalizing kiss.

No. She wouldn't let that happen. Unlike everything else, her response to this infuriating man was something she could still control.

Lara tightened her grip around the sheet. "Why did you lock me in here?"

"For your own protection. I didn't want you running naked through the streets again."

She shook her head, not buying it. "You came in while I slept and uncuffed me. You knew the effects of the curse were gone by that time. Why did you lock the door again?"

Tristan's lips twitched at the corners and he tilted his head, watching her with something akin to grudging admiration. "Because I didn't think you'd stay if I asked nicely."

She opened her mouth to argue but knew it was futile. He was right. She wouldn't have stayed. She took a deep breath and tried a different approach. "Where did you go?"

"I met with Julian Smith tonight."

"Illiana's brother?"

He leaned closer, his eyes sparkling with uncontained excitement. "That's him."

He told her about finding Julian singing in a hole-in-the-wall bar, about their conversation outside and Julian's dismissal. Then he told her about sending him to Richard at Bitter Sweet.

No matter how hard Lara wanted to hold her anger to her chest like a protective shield, it dissipated with each rich intonation of his voice.

He continually surprised her. She wouldn't have expected a man such as Tristan to give up his one advantage over the owner of the most popular club in New York for the good of another. Especially for a man he didn't know, a man who couldn't repay him in return.

Tristan reached out and twirled one of her curls between his fingers. "A few days ago, I wouldn't have."

She knew she hadn't spoken aloud, but her wonder must have been significant enough that he'd heard her thought. She met his gaze, her heart hammering wildly in her chest. "What's changed?"

"You." He swept his thumb over her lower lip. "You've changed me."

His hand caressed her throat as he leaned in to brush his mouth over hers. The kiss was infinitely gentle, feather soft. It sent a tremor through Lara's body and she wrapped her hand around his neck, pulling him to her, arching against him.

The nightmare still lingered in the distant recesses of her mind but it held no power in the waking world. Not anymore. Not when Tristan's arms were around her. Not when the hard planes of his chest pressed against her breasts, sending a jolt of arousal to travel a slick path to her pussy.

Not when she could no longer fight what her heart had been telling her from the beginning.

The curse wanted to keep them apart, but even the strongest magic, the kind with the power over life and death, couldn't pry Lara from Tristan's side for long.

She'd never believed in soul mates before. The concept that there was only one person out there for everyone wasn't just absurd, it was downright scary. What if she never found that person? Would she be doomed to wander the world alone?

Yet now as Lara savored the taste of Tristan, minty and slightly metallic, she knew without a doubt she'd found her mate.

Mine.

He chuckled against her mouth. His hand slid lower to brush against the swell of her breast. She sucked in a breath, *his* breath, and ran her tongue across his, seeking, exploring, needing to feel every nuance of his arousal.

When they broke apart, she leaned her forehead against his and trailed her fingertips over his jaw. "I'm sorry you didn't learn anything new from Julian. What you did for him though..." She bit her lip and shook her head slightly. "It was incredibly selfless."

He pulled back, golden shadows painting chestnut highlights in his long hair and glinting off his fangs. "Who said I didn't learn anything new?"

For a moment, she thought she hadn't heard him correctly. "But you said he left after saying he had no other relatives in the city who would know anything about the curse."

"That's true. But then he remembered a crazy great-aunt who lives on the outskirts of London. She dabbles in love potions and the like." He raised an eyebrow. "If anyone would know something about a lust-triggered curse cast by an ancestor, she would."

Lara gnawed on her lower lip, unable to breathe, unwilling to hope.

Tristan brushed a curl away from her face and tucked it behind her ear. "I'm going to London. I'll talk to this woman and I'll get us some real answers. Hey." He tipped her chin up so she had to look into his eyes. The tenderness she saw there melted her heart. "You're going to be okay. We'll beat this thing."

His certainty was contagious. Lara released a long sigh then shook her head and reached for his hand, twining her fingers with his. "You're right. *We* will."

Tristan narrowed his eyes. "Why don't I like the sound of that?"

Lara shrugged. "I'm coming with you."

Tristan opened his mouth but Lara was quicker. She pressed two fingers against his lips, silencing his protest. "Before you say anything, just listen. This curse affects me more than it affects you. I trust you with my life but I want to be involved in the search for a cure." She swallowed hard. "No, that's not true. I *need* to be involved. I can't sit by idly while you take care of me. I've done too much of that over the years." She saw his jaw clench at the comparison to her father and brother but pressed on. "I'm not a child, Tristan. I'm not helpless. You may be stronger and quicker but I'm just as fiercely determined to find a way to stop this curse as you are. Maybe more so."

With nothing more to say, Lara leaned back against the headrest and waited. She'd done it. She'd said her piece. Now it was up to him.

"Okay."

"You haven't thought this through. I can help you — " She paused in mid-sentence, his response only then making sense. "Wait. You said yes? You'll take me with you to London?"

He grinned. "If I left you here, I'd spend all my time worrying you'd find a way to pick the lock using a pair of handcuffs."

She swatted his shoulder playfully. "I could have, given enough time."

"Besides, you'll get to meet my brother."

"Hayden?" Her pussy clenched at the dream memory of his talented tongue sweeping through her folds. She hoped her face didn't reflect the heat rushing through her body. "I've already met him."

Tristan shook his head. "No. Alexander, our youngest brother. I told you he lives in London."

Suddenly, the trip no longer sounded like such a good idea. Dealing with one Chance man was difficult enough. Judging by her dreams, two had proven a real challenge to her overactive imagination, not to mention her ardent libido.

Sure, she was now convinced she and Tristan were meant to be together but that didn't mean the blazing lust raging through her veins could be appeased by that simple knowledge.

Three gorgeous Chance brothers in close proximity might prove too much to handle, even for her.

She sat up, determined to ignore the wetness smearing her cunt. "When do we leave?"

Chapter Twelve

ॐ

Walking into Midwich felt like stepping back through time. A chill wind blew from the north, stirring the sparkling blanket of snow into the cool night air.

"Are you sure this is the right place?" Lara asked, glancing at the crumbling stone around her. The houses looked ancient, built from solid rock that stood gray and foreboding against the night sky. She saw no hint of electricity. No light blazed from any of the windows and there were no streetlights to illuminate their way.

Only the silver moon, hanging full and heavy between glittering stars set like diamonds in the dark sky, sent a rippling wave of light over the village.

"I'm sure." Tristan squeezed her hand. "While you slept, I took the time to do some research on the mysterious Annabelle Doherty."

Hayden's deep chuckle slid down Lara's skin, making her shiver. "Let me guess… She has a website all set up, freely offering curses and cures to anyone with a laptop and an Internet connection."

Moonlight glinted off Tristan's fangs as he scowled at his brother. "Not exactly. I had a hell of a time finding any information on this village at all. It's as if this is the last place on earth untouched by modern technology. It doesn't even show up on Google Maps."

"But it has a landing strip," Lara pointed out, hitching her thumb over her shoulder in the direction of the flat ribbon of land behind them.

"It's odd," Tristan agreed, "But I don't think that space was meant to be used as a landing site for private jets."

A shiver ran down Lara's spine, and she wasn't sure it was due entirely to the cold winter wind. "What did you discover?"

"In the end, I managed to find the phone number for the local church. I spoke to the town pastor, who told me where we can find Annabelle's shop. He also warned us not to expect much from her. He said she hasn't exactly been lucid lately."

Lara blew out a breath. "So she's insane. That's just great."

"This is such a waste of time," Hayden mumbled under his breath. Lara stiffened. If she'd heard his angry whisper, Tristan would have too.

"Do you have a better idea?" Tristan uttered the words without inflection but the threat behind them was clear.

Hayden didn't answer. From the corner of her eye, Lara saw him shake his head.

Together they rounded a bend at the end of the road and turned onto a narrow path. The houses were sparser here. Behind them, a dark, foreboding forest cast deep shadows over the snowy ground.

Just as the pastor had said, they found Annabelle's house at the far edge of the village. The simple one-floor stone structure stood alone, set apart from the other houses in a circular meadow. Beyond it, the woods loomed immense, like an army of silent sentinels keeping eternal watch over Annabelle Doherty as she slept.

A wooden sign hanging outside the door welcomed customers to The Bay Leaf. Three stone steps led to a narrow porch. To the left of the stairs stood a single stone bench. Images had been elaborately carved in the rock but Lara couldn't make out what they depicted from where she stood.

The flickering ripple of candlelight wavered in the far right window. "You think she's still awake?" Lara asked.

"It's only a few minutes past midnight," Tristan said. "And if she's not, she will be soon."

He walked up the steps, his shoes leaving deep imprints in the fresh snow. Lara followed and stood by his side as he knocked on the door. Hayden remained ten steps away, hands shoved deep in the pockets of his leather jacket.

There was no answer to Tristan's knock and no shuffling sound echoed from within. He tried again to no avail.

"I can come back in the morning," Lara offered.

Tristan scowled. "I'll be damned if I'm leaving before I see this woman." He grasped the doorknob. It turned easily in his hand.

The hinge emitted a sharp metal squeak as Tristan pushed the door open.

Lara grimaced. "Hello? Is anyone here? Annabelle?"

They stepped over the threshold into a surprisingly large room. It was modestly decorated with an old-fashioned round wooden table and four matching chairs as the centerpiece. Against one wall stood a chunky wooden bookshelf filled with leather-bound tomes and myriad jars holding everything from parsley and coriander to unusual orange and bright blue powders. Rugs woven in bright colors covered the stone floor and elaborate weavings hung on the walls.

Lara cleared her throat and tried again. "Annabelle? Are you here? We just want to talk."

A deep, encompassing silence answered her call. Lara's gut knotted. She turned to Tristan and grabbed his arm, leaning close into the strong, reassuring feel of his body. "Maybe we scared her, barging in here in the middle of the night."

Before Tristan could answer, sparkles floated in Lara's field of vision. Golden flecks clung to her skin and fell to the ground, scattering like tiny fireflies before her. She looked up, for the first time noticing the wooden rafters that ran around the beams supporting the roof.

An old woman leaned against a rafter, blowing the sparkling dust from her palm onto Lara and Tristan. Her wrinkled skin drooped from a thin, almost skeletal face but her luminous blue eyes shone brightly with awareness.

"Sweet dreams," the crone whispered, a moment before Lara's legs folded beneath her and the stone floor rushed up to meet her.

* * * * *

"You came."

Katherine Smith clung to the doorframe, trembling with barely contained excitement. Calvin Chance stood before her, beaming a crooked grin. Her heart skipped a beat.

"You knew I would."

She swallowed hard. When she'd added the final ingredient to the love potion she'd intended to slip into his drink, she'd allowed herself a moment of guilty hesitation. A lifetime's worth of knowledge on differentiating between right and wrong told her enticing a man into her bed, stripping him of his free will simply for her own pleasure was vile and depraved.

And yet all her lectures on morality couldn't convince her to not spill the brew into Calvin's drink when he came to the tavern after sunset that night.

She opened the door wider and watched his lean frame appreciatively as he stepped inside her humble home. The latch of the bolt drawing closed resonated through the room with a heart-stopping finality, as though she'd just sealed her fate.

Taking a deep breath, Katherine spun around and collided with Calvin's broad chest. "Oh," she murmured, a hot flush creeping over her cheeks as she felt his erection prodding her stomach.

He reached out and pressed his palm against the small of her back, eliminating every bit of space between them. His breath warmed her neck. "You asked me here for a reason," he whispered, his voice soft and infinitely arousing.

"Yes," she murmured over the frantic pounding of her heart. Her thoughts reeled with the nearness of him.

For ten years she'd loved him from afar. She'd watched him grow from a youth into a man and she'd suffered in silence as he chased after every woman in town.

Every woman but her.

She'd cried herself to sleep countless nights, wishing he'd warm her bed, her home, her life. And yet no matter how much she desperately hoped he'd turn his smoky gaze her way, he hadn't. Nor had he settled down, taken a wife. Rumor had it he spent enough time with other men's wives to know he didn't want one of his own, but Katherine believed the truth was simpler than that. He simply hadn't been with his soul mate yet.

One night with her and he'd change his mind. But it was taking him too long to realize that what he sought had been right in front of him the entire time and she'd grown tired of waiting.

If Calvin wasn't going to come to her willingly, Katherine was determined to do anything in her power to draw him to her, through any means necessary. And now here he was, ready and willing, determined to finally stop wandering blindly through life and take hold of his destiny.

Katherine tilted her head, her lips barely brushing his. "I'm yours."

He captured her mouth, his tongue slipping between her lips and sending an array of wild sensations coursing down her body. She wrapped her arms around his neck, pulling him closer. Her breasts flattened against his chest but her nipples beaded, tightly budding through the coarse material of her apron.

He tasted like ale, the slightly bitter aroma seeping into her mouth. She didn't care. She'd watched his lips make contact with the stein too many nights, wishing his mouth was devouring her instead. She'd taken the work offered her at the tavern because she knew that was where he went, night after night, after a long day of toiling at the blacksmiths' shop.

It was worth every coarse gesture, every rude invite from the regular patrons just to watch Calvin stride into the tavern at the end of a long day. Now she no longer had to content herself with watching him from afar. He was here, in her house, in her arms, and she was never going to let him go.

He tugged on the knot tying her apron with expert fingers and she felt the material loosen around her waist. She shrugged out of it, her mouth never leaving his. Her ankle-length skirt came off next, leaving her standing before him in nothing but her white shirt and bare feet.

Her sex clenched, moisture coating the swollen lips. She'd touched herself intimately, knew enough about her own pleasure to know what to expect but still she trembled as he broke the kiss and stood back, his steely gaze scrutinizing every inch of her.

"Take it off," he commanded, and with shaking fingers she drew the garment over her head then dropped it on the floor. She sank her teeth into her lower lip and lowered her eyes, unable to take any more of his intense perusal.

A moment passed then another. Katherine watched his feet as he shed his shoes. She saw his trousers pool in a mass of fabric. Heat sizzled along her nerve endings. When she finally mustered the courage to look up again, he stood before her naked, his body more magnificent than she'd ever imagined.

Her gaze scanned every groove, every plane and lean line of muscle. She drank him in, unable to get enough. She focused on his arms, darkly tanned and muscular. She eyed his chest, the luscious, inviting duskiness of his male nipples. Then she glanced lower, at the flat abdomen and the thin trail of hair leading to his massive shaft.

She couldn't help the gasp that echoed from her lips. She'd heard enough about male anatomy to know what to expect but the hard ridge of his cock both surprised and dismayed her. The shaft was long, too long to fit inside her, Katherine thought. He was thick too, as wide across as four of her fingers held side by side.

"Don't be frightened." Calvin closed the distance between them. His work-roughened hands slid up her waist to cup her breasts.

She inhaled sharply at the sensation spearing her sex and fought the urge to rub her thighs together. God above, but he was even more talented than she'd expected. Her head reeled from the new sensations flooding every nerve ending. How could any woman resist his touch? No wonder he'd had his pick of women in the village.

She dismissed that thought, determined not to stray down that path. After tonight, Calvin was going to be hers—forever. Though the effects of the love potion would wear off shortly and remain her dark secret for the rest of her days. But it wouldn't matter. As soon as he slipped his rod into her, he'd know he'd found Heaven. She had no doubt they were meant to be together. Destiny couldn't be fought, couldn't be denied.

He palmed her breast, toying with her nipple. Tension knotted her stomach but she succumbed to the flood of heat drenching her sex and leaned in to gently nip the skin of his shoulder. Her boldness gave her courage. His skin tasted like sweat and what she imagined lust would taste like if it had a flavor. Salty and decidedly masculine, it lingered on her tongue.

She dipped her head lower, trailing her tongue down the muscular lines of his chest, drowning in his heady perfume.

"Katherine," he whispered, his voice hoarse with need.

She kneeled before him, firmly intending not to think about what she was going to do before she did it. His cock speared the air before him, proud and erect. A bead of wetness slid from the slick tip, dripping down the length of his shaft. She caught it on a fingertip and smeared it over his rock-hard manhood.

Calvin rewarded her with a shudder, and for the first time, she realized she had the power to affect him as well. She smiled as she tentatively swept the tip of her tongue over the tiny slit of his cock.

Calvin groaned. He reached for her hair and tangled his fingers in it, shoving her head closer to his straining staff. Encouraged, she welcomed his sex into her mouth. He thrust his hips and the head nudged the back of her throat, making her gag. Still, he pressed her head to his groin. Her eyes watered from the intrusion clogging her throat. She blinked back the tears and sucked boldly.

She'd spoken to enough women who'd had the pleasure of bedding him to know what he liked, what he wanted. They'd all told her this particular act turned him on unlike any other and she was determined to bring him ecstasy as he'd never experienced.

Her nails grazed his sac. Calvin sucked in a breath and released it on a hiss, his hips moving in rhythm with her mouth. She fondled his balls, cradling them in her palm and applying gentle pressure to the soft tissue below the opening to his anus.

Unexpectedly, he pulled her head back. She stumbled backward but he held her still. She looked up and found his eyes narrowed, glancing down at her with a dark, lust-filled gaze.

"Stand," he ordered.

She pressed a kiss to his inner thigh before obeying.

"I want you to feel my cock inside you. To take it all in your tight, hot sex."

He led her to the pallet by the blazing hearth. The flames sent a steady heat toward them and hot air feathered across her already overheated skin. Despite the warmth, Katherine trembled as she lay down and spread her legs.

Calvin moved between her parted thighs. He slicked his fingers in the moisture coating the entrance to her sex then slid them inside her. She gasped at the unexpected intrusion.

"I don't usually tumble with virgins," he told her in a quiet voice. "But you're not like the others, are you? You won't scream when I enter you."

Katherine shook her head, silently praying she wouldn't let him down. He was so much more experienced than she was. At almost thirty, she was likely the last woman in all of England not to have lain with a man.

But she'd saved herself. She'd waited many long years.

For him.

He pressed the tip of her cock to the entrance of her channel and she stiffened, expecting the pain to come and preparing to brace it without a sound. It would be over in a flash, Katherine silently promised herself, and then she could give her body and soul over entirely to the ecstasy his touch ignited.

His cock slipped inside her wet sex. He went slowly, but when it came, the spearing pain ran straight through her body. She bit the inside of her cheek as tears welled in her eyes. She wouldn't cry out. She *wouldn't*.

Calvin smiled and her heart skipped a beat. She forgot about the hurt as he began to move inside her, hot and hard, filling her. She'd expected his staff to be too large for her to accommodate but she found her inner muscles squeezed him and her entrance adjusted to the intrusion with ease.

They were made for each other, just as she'd always known. Now he had all the physical proof he needed too.

Each stroke took him deeper inside her. His thrusts filled her to capacity. She clung to his shoulders, her fingernails digging into his skin, never wanting to let go.

Her tender nipples grazed against his chest as he bent his head and slid his tongue inside her mouth. His cock pounded at her core, his thrusts growing frenzied as his cries of passion filled the room. Her sex quivered, succumbing to the myriad sensations streaming through her.

Colors flashed behind Katherine's eyelids as her release slammed into her, making her inner walls clench in ecstasy. Calvin followed, his grunts growing more adamant. He stilled inside her and she felt the hot stream of his seed flood her sex.

Calvin grunted and rolled off her. "My lord, that was better than I could have dreamed." Katherine knew she was beaming but she couldn't help it. They'd stepped right into fate's decree, playing the parts history had ordained for them.

And then in a sudden, blinding flash, destiny unraveled around her.

"Mmm, well, I must go." Calvin stood and reached for his trousers.

For a moment, Katherine couldn't muster the energy to move. Then sudden understanding flooded her veins and she bolted upright. "You're not staying." She forced the words through lips that felt thick and numb.

He turned toward her, all the tenderness she'd seen in his countenance having vanished. Or perhaps she'd only imagined it there all along.

"I can't. Mary is waiting."

"Mary Connor? The seamstress?"

He shrugged. "She's expecting me."

Katherine's heart shredded into a million pieces as the world collapsed around her. "You can't. Not after..." Tears clogged her throat. "Not now."

Calvin cupped his groin through his trousers. "You pleased me, Katherine. I don't know what took me so long to sample your wares. Perhaps I'll come to you again tomorrow."

Your wares. She flinched away from the smug tone in his voice. He spoke as though she sold her body as she would a loaf of bread or a mug of ale.

Wetness flooded Katherine's cheeks. A hundred arguments clogged her throat but no sound escaped her lips as Calvin walked through the door. She didn't run after him or throw herself at his feet as perhaps she should have done. Maybe then he'd have stayed. Maybe then...

No.

He hadn't wanted her. He'd never cared for her beyond fulfilling his needs.

Moisture dripped down her thigh as she rose from the bed. She looked down at the smear of her virgin blood against her pale skin. Trembling, she walked to the small altar she'd made from colored rocks. Lowering her head she prayed—the only way she knew how.

"Heavenly Mother, hear me. As long as the Chance line continues to create male heirs, none shall partake of their true mates. They shall have to endure meaningless encounters, to be denied the one woman who can make them complete." She wiped the back of her hand over her cheek then continued. "The woman, the life mate, shall fare no better."

Why should she? Katherine was doomed to a life of loneliness. As a deflowered old maid, she would suffer for the rest of her days.

She'd rather be dead.

Unless...

Katherine took a deep breath and placed her palm over her stomach. "The Chance heir shall have seven days to proclaim his love. But the true test will lie where it counts the most. In his seed. Only the quickening in his mate's womb will save her life...and his future."

Chapter Thirteen

ஓ

Tristan could only watch helplessly as Lara crumpled to the floor. Glowing dust formed a cocoon around her body, enveloping her in sparkling shades of gold.

"What have you done, old woman?" Tristan shouted, dropping to his knees beside Lara's fallen form.

He gathered her body and drew her to his chest, fear sending a jolt of adrenaline through his system. He'd be damned if he'd let her die. He hadn't traveled all this way to find a cure for the curse only to watch the woman he loved perish before his eyes.

He'd do whatever it took to keep that from happening, even if it meant tearing Annabelle Doherty apart limb by limb.

Tristan's muscles stiffened as he bent his head to Lara's chest. He held his breath, listening for the sound of blood rushing through her veins. Relief swept through his body and pooled low in his stomach at the sound of the steady pulsing flow. He could feel her heartbeat, steady and reassuring, and he allowed himself to release a deep, shuddering breath.

Lara's eyelashes fluttered.

"I'm here, baby." Tristan trailed his fingertips over her cheek.

A tear escaped from beneath Lara's eyelids then another and another, but she gave no indication of waking.

Panic welled in Tristan's chest. "What's happening?" He glanced up at the rafters but Annabelle was gone.

A thick layer of golden dust had settled over Lara's features, casting an unnatural metallic sheen over her deathly pale face. The tears left bold streaks through the dust and Tristan wiped the moisture away with the back of his hand.

Lara's entire body trembled with silent sobs, making his heart clench. He shook her gently. "Wake up, honey. You're okay. Wake up."

She blinked slowly. He held his breath, unwilling to move for fear she'd breathe her last in his arms. When she opened her eyes and looked at him, relief poured through his veins.

Lara's dark, luminous orbs shone with a deep, heartbreaking sorrow that made his heart clench in his chest. She licked her lips. The tip of her tongue removed some of the gold particles, revealing the luscious crimson of her mouth. "I know how to end the curse," she said, her voice barely above a whisper.

Tristan sucked in a breath. "That's wonderful."

She gave him a shaky smile and tried to rise but he tightened his hold around her. He wasn't ready to let her go. After the scare she'd given him, he wasn't sure he ever would be.

As she attempted to get up, her ass wiggled against his groin, making his cock jolt to awareness. He stifled a groan.

"It's great," she said. "If you like babies."

"Babies?" he echoed stupidly. "I don't understand."

"She's right." The words sounded steeped in time, as though echoing from a great distance. Tristan looked up and met the old woman's eyes. She stood a few steps away, leaning against the stone mantel of the hearth.

"Annabelle, I assume." Anger turned Tristan's voice cold.

The crone tilted her head. Piercing blue eyes assessed him coolly. "Indeed. And you must be a Chance heir."

"If you know who I am, then you know why we're here. Tell us what we have to do to end the curse."

"No need," Lara said. "Katherine already told me everything I need to know."

Tristan frowned. "Katherine Smith? The woman who cast the curse? How?"

Lara shook her head. "I don't know exactly. But I saw her. No, that's not right. I *felt* her. I know why she thought she was justified in doing what she did. Frankly, I can't quite say I blame her."

Tristan rose to his feet, still holding Lara. He glanced from her to Annabelle. "Is one of you going to let me in on the big secret?"

Lara ran the tip of her thumb over his lower lip. He resisted the urge to draw it into his mouth.

"Hell hath no fury like a woman scorned," she whispered softly. "Calvin Chance used her. I'm sure it wasn't the first time a man slept with a woman purely for his own pleasure but Katherine gave herself to him body and soul. And he stomped all over her heart."

"So she cursed his entire bloodline," Tristan said.

"Precisely," Annabelle answered. "She believed any man sired by Calvin Chance would be unworthy of finding true love. At least until he proved otherwise."

Tristan looked down at the woman in his arms. Raw emotion sent a sweet, searing warmth pouring through his veins. "I do love you." The words tumbled forth from his lips, surprising him with their vehemence.

Lara ran her fingers through his hair. A sad smile curved the corners of her lips. "I believe you. But it's not enough."

"Then I'll prove it in any way I need to. Especially if it means saving your life."

She flattened her palms against his chest. "Put me down. I need to be standing when I tell you this."

He did as she asked, his jaw clenched tightly. He had a feeling he wasn't going to like what she had to tell him.

Lara opened her mouth to speak then closed it again. She took a deep breath and spun on her heel to face Annabelle. "What happened to Katherine?"

The old woman lifted a jar from the mantel. It held a viscous red liquid that coated the translucent glass. She peered inside it, as though it held the answer to Lara's question. "She waited until she was sure she wasn't with child. Then she took her own life."

Lara sighed. She turned toward Tristan and reached out to caress his face but dropped her hand a moment before she made contact with his skin. "It seems the only way to end this curse is to get me pregnant."

For a moment, Tristan thought he hadn't heard right. Then all the comfort he'd taken from knowing they'd reached the end of their journey shattered into a million pieces.

Like his heart.

"I can't." The admission pained him more than he'd have thought possible.

Lara stared at him, hurt and puzzled. "You don't want to have a child with me?"

From where she stood, Annabelle snorted. "True to his blood. No surprise there."

Tristan clenched his hands into fists at his sides. Rage poured through his body, cording his muscles. "No. That's not it. I physically cannot get a woman pregnant. My kind doesn't procreate as we once used to. Humanity's rules no longer apply."

Comprehension dawned in Lara's eyes. Tristan expected panic to follow. Instead, her eyes shone with a strange kind of acceptance. "This is it then. I'm going to die and there's nothing either of us can do about it."

"Not true," Annabelle said, pointing at him. "He can change that, if he chooses."

Tristan gritted his teeth. He was growing tired of the old woman's interruptions. Her assessment of him left a lot to be desired.

"I just explained this to you," Tristan said with all the patience he could muster. "It's not possible."

The crone lifted a skeletal shoulder in a half shrug. "Vampires sire other vampires. You may not use the same process but the result is close enough that it will satisfy Katherine's condition."

Tristan took a step back. Old pain came rushing back, uncovering wounds he'd thought long buried. He shook his head. "No. I won't put anyone through that again. Never again."

Lara stared at him wide-eyed. "You're talking about turning me into a vampire."

Memories of his wife's death had haunted Tristan for centuries. He'd vowed after turning her he'd never watch another woman suffer as she had. "It's not going to happen. There must be another way."

"There is no other way," Annabelle said. "Katherine wanted to ensure you were worthy of the woman's love. And she knew that living without you would cause her unbearable pain, so she wanted to avoid that too. Either you create a permanent bond between you or your beloved dies."

"I already watched one woman die because she couldn't handle living the way I do. Drinking blood. Never seeing another sunrise again for all eternity. I won't force Lara down the same path."

"Don't you love me enough to let me make up my own mind?" Lara, her face still smudged with gold and streaked with tears, crossed the distance between them. She wrapped her arms around his neck and pressed her lips to his.

The salty flavor of her tears melded with her own unique taste. It slid into his mouth, weakening his resolve. Her tongue swept between his lips, brushing against his. A blazing wave of arousal rushed into his groin. He groaned into her mouth and slid his palms down her back. Cupping her ass, he pulled her to him, crushing her full breasts against his chest.

At last she broke away. Her breath warmed his lips. "All my life, I've yearned for the kind of love I've found in your arms. And now you're threatening to take that away from me because you don't think I know what I want."

He saw the faith and determination in her gaze. It awed him, as did her courage. "Do you know what you're committing yourself to? An existence—"

She silenced him by vehemently shaking her head. "I'm agreeing to spending eternity by your side. The alternative is death in…two days. How can you deny me the choice?"

Tristan sucked in a breath. How could he indeed?

After only a moment's hesitation, Tristan nodded, praying he wouldn't regret this. "We'll need Hayden and Alexander. They must agree to the turning as well."

Lara's mouth parted in surprise. Was it just his imagination or did her pulse quicken at the mention of his brothers' names?

"Why?" she asked.

"The making of a vampire isn't a simple task. It's a blood union. As such, every member of that bloodline must participate in the turning process. You won't just have one sire. You'll have three."

She swallowed hard then slid her hand into his. "Then let's ask them."

Tristan activated the telepathic link to his brother, who had remained outside. Before he could explain what had happened, Hayden's unease slid through their bond, making Tristan's pulse race.

What's going on? Tristan asked.

I don't know. Shadows are moving through the edges of the forest, so silent I can't hear them. Something's not right.

Tristan tightened his grip on Lara's hand and half guided, half dragged her behind him. "We have to go."

"What's wrong?"

Tristan didn't answer. Adrenaline pumped through his veins, setting his heightened senses on alert. He listened, hearing nothing but the whisper of the wind. Like Hayden, he now felt the added presence lurking in the forest.

He'd almost reached his brother's side when the first attack struck.

The bullet whizzed through the air, its aim unwavering. Tristan had only a moment to react, but a moment was long enough. He shoved his brother to the ground and pushed Lara down on top of Hayden. "Don't move!"

"Like hell!" Faster than thought, Hayden was on his feet.

Another bullet hissed close to Tristan's ear. He ducked low, his eyes narrowing as he scanned the perimeter of the forest. Then he saw them—three shadows floating like misty wraiths broke from the deeper darkness bordering the meadow.

He opened his mouth to shout a warning but the words didn't have time to leave his lips before a powerful slam smashed him up against the thick trunk of a nearby tree.

Pain exploded in his chest. A hand wrapped around his neck, pinning him to the tree. The attacker wasn't human, Tristan realized through a dizzying fog of unfamiliar fear.

Vampire, Hayden shouted in his mind.

It all made a crazy kind of sense. The assassination attempt in Florida. The silver bullets.

Lara, Tristan sent back by way of an answer. *Where is she?*

Hayden didn't answer and not knowing frightened Tristan more than anything his brother could have said. A tight, spiraling knot formed deep inside him. He summoned up all the rage he'd felt over his inability to protect Lara from the curse and poured it into a counterattack.

He shoved, kicked and pummeled at the vampire holding him. His arms shot up and he wrapped his hands around the man's neck, their moves mirroring each other. Moonlight glinted off his enemy's fangs.

Tristan tightened his hold around the vampire's neck and felt his own fangs extend in response to the violent stimuli flooding the air. The scent of blood teased his nostrils with its coppery aroma. An unfamiliar wave of pure terror flooded Tristan's veins.

Lara! He tried again to send the thought to his brother but received nothing in return. In fact, he *felt* nothing. Not even a hint of Hayden's emotions, which he should have been able to pick up on in a whim in such close proximity to his blood kin.

He's down.

The unexpected answer sent a jolt of relief and renewed energy into Tristan. He brought his knee up and felt it connect with his opponent's groin. The vampire snarled, his fangs snapping perilously close to Tristan's neck.

Alexander. The woman – Lara. Find her. Protect her.

The pause that followed was unbearable. A scream rend the air—a woman's voice. Tristan's heart hammered in his chest and he tore himself free of his attacker. He looked around the meadow wildly and saw a second vampire hurl Lara toward the edge of the meadow. Alexander leapt and caught her in midair.

Done.

His youngest brother joining the fray lent a fresh rush of rampant frenzy to the fight. Raw, primal anger ripped a cry from Tristan's throat.

His muscles stiffened and he lunged, no longer caring about anything but ending the threat to his blood kin and to Lara.

He landed a sharp jab against the vampire's ribs. A moment later, he kicked the back of his attacker's knees and watched as the man collapsed facedown toward the ground.

Inhumanly fast, his opponent's hands shot out to catch him. He rebounded, leaping into the air and returning Tristan's furious cry with a snarl of his own.

The battle continued to rage around them. Blood stained the white snow, dark and glistening in the silver moonlight.

Tristan dashed forward, catching the vampire off guard as he raced past him and turned at the last moment to grip him around the neck. His fangs sank into the man's throat and he pulled, tearing a chunk of flesh. He spat then dove in for another attack and another, until blood ran unheeded down his chin and the vampire's limbs no longer supported his weight.

A flash of barely perceived light dashed through the air. Alexander came to a stop beside him, his hand wrapped around a wooden stake, which he plunged downward toward the vampire's heart.

Tristan's arm shot out, intercepting the blow. "Not yet."

Alexander gritted his teeth. His green eyes flashed in warning. "If we don't kill him, he'll kill us."

"I know."

He took the stake from Alexander's hand and held it over the vampire's chest. "One wrong answer and you're dead."

The attacker brought his hand to his neck. Blood trickled through his fingers. "I'm dead anyway," he said, the words barely discernable through the gaping hole that held his mangled vocal cords.

"Who sent you?"

For a moment, Tristan thought the vampire wouldn't answer. Then the man licked his lips and gestured almost imperceptibly toward the edge of the meadow. Tristan followed his gaze and saw Lara kneeling over Hayden's fallen form. Two other vampire corpses lay crumpled around them.

Hayden's body was horribly, unbearably still.

"Ask her." The vampire sneered.

"Lara." Tristan shook his head. "It's not possible that she put you up to this."

"Not directly. Though she must have known."

Understanding slammed into Tristan's chest. "Her father."

"Yesss," the vampire hissed, a low and angry sound. "And if we don't succeed, someone else will. The Sanctuary takes its vows seriously."

With all the supernatural force he possessed, Tristan slammed the stake home. It crunched through bone and found the organ it sought, plunging through the vampire's heart. Blood gushed through the surface, soaking the fabric of the man's shirt and seeping into the ground.

Alexander pulled Tristan to his feet. Together they ran to Hayden and Lara.

She looked up, her eyes swimming with tears. She held her hands pressed over a wound in Hayden's throat. The lesion gaped beneath her slim fingers. "I can't stop the bleeding."

Alexander shoved her aside, not unkindly. "Let me."

Tristan watched as his brother tore the vein in his wrist and positioned the rush of blood to flow into Hayden's mouth. For a moment, nothing happened. Then Hayden lurched forward, his lips molding around Alexander's wrist.

Lara stood on shaky legs. Tristan drew her to his side, relishing the way her firm curves pressed against his body. Heat emanated from her skin, arousing and reassuring at once.

At last Hayden released Alexander's wrist. Tristan watched as the flesh kneaded and his brother's wounds drew closed.

Releasing a deep breath, Tristan gestured at the wooden stake protruding from the nearest dead vampire's chest. "Still hunting rogues, I see."

Alexander shrugged. "It's my job. Besides, someone has to. The Sanctuary of Fallen Vampires has only grown stronger in the past two decades. They have new leadership, I hear. Their powers have increased and they've become bolder. They're even hiring themselves out to those who seek their services." He ran his hand through his short hair, his brows furrowing over his eyes. "If you knew you were going to have company, you should have told me. I would have been here sooner."

"Looks to me like you came just in time," Tristan said.

Alexander nodded, his gaze sweeping over the protective way Tristan held on to Lara. "And the night's not over yet, is it?"

Tristan grimaced. Alexander had always been too perceptive for his own good. Even when they were kids, Tristan had never been able to hide anything from him for long.

Hayden rose to his feet, the slick blood staining his white shirt the only reminder that his throat had been torn apart only minutes earlier. "What's he talking about?"

Despite everything that had happened, Tristan couldn't help the excitement that surged through his body, hardening his cock. "I found a way to end the curse."

Hayden's eyes widened. A flash of sadness flickered over his face. A moment later, it disappeared as quickly as it emerged. "Good. That's...very, very good."

Alexander raised an eyebrow at the mention of the family curse but didn't interrupt as Tristan filled them both in on what had happened inside Annabelle's house.

"It was that simple all along?" Hayden shook his head. "I didn't know. I—"

"You couldn't have known," Tristan interrupted. "Lara was the key to learning the truth behind the curse."

"But Annabelle knew. I should have found her sooner. She'd have told me everything."

Lara placed a hand on Hayden's arm. "Perhaps. Then again, her nephew believed she was senile. Maybe she would have acted like a raving lunatic and pretended to have no knowledge of the curse. If you'd brought your mate, perhaps she might have seen the circumstances that prompted Katherine's dire act."

"Tell us," Hayden said, taking a step closer. "Tell us what you saw."

Lara took a deep, shuddering breath and released it on a sigh. When she began speaking, the brothers stood by her side, riveted to her every word. She described the events as they unfolded and when she finished, she glanced at each brother in turn. "So what happens now?"

"Now, my dear," Hayden said, taking her hand and bringing it to his lips. "You become one of us."

Chapter Fourteen

ဢ

Fear snaked down Lara's spine for the first time since the vampires attacked. Then, she'd acted on instinct and pure adrenaline. She hadn't even had time to panic when she found herself hurled through the air and landed in a pair of strong, masculine and oddly comforting arms.

She knew immediately that the man who held her wasn't one of the attackers. One look at his full, sensuous lips, his straight nose, his dark hair and the firm line of his jaw, and she knew she was looking at Alexander Chance, Tristan's youngest brother.

Hayden's palm was cold around her hand and not just from the chill winter breeze. His lips made contact with her skin and she shivered, emotions warring inside her.

What had she just agreed to?

She didn't know anything about the turning process. Would it hurt? Would it take long? Would she still be herself when it was over and her cells had adapted to their new state of perpetual undeath?

"Hey." Tristan's breath caressed her cheek. He cupped the back of her neck and kneaded the muscles there with his strong fingers. "You okay?"

She pulled her hand from Hayden's and bunched her fingers into a fist at her side. It was too late to change her mind now, even if she wanted to.

"I'm fine." She tilted her head and met Tristan's lips for a fleeting kiss. The soft contact replaced the chill in her blood with searing heat that pounded a path straight to her pussy.

"If we're going to do this tonight, we have to do it soon," Alexander said. "It will be dawn in a couple of hours."

"Your place then?" Hayden suggested. "I didn't see a hotel in the village when we walked through."

"There isn't one." Annabelle's voice seemed to come from nowhere and everywhere at once. Lara darted a glance in the direction of the house. The old woman stood a few steps away, leaning on a gnarled walking stick. "You'll never complete the turning before dawn. You could wait until tomorrow, but why put this off any longer than you must? Unless you're questioning the wisdom of the decision you've made."

From the corner of her eye, Lara saw Tristan scowl. "I suppose you have a better idea?"

Annabelle inclined her head. "Use Katherine's cottage."

A gasp broke free from Lara's throat before she could stop it. "She—you—wouldn't mind?"

"Katherine would have wanted the first Chance heir to break her curse to do so within the walls of her home." Annabelle's voice dropped to a low murmur and Lara had to strain to make out the words. "I hear her sometimes, drifting through, always watching, waiting for her beloved to see the error of his ways and return to her. Calvin will never come but perhaps seeing you perform your ritual will give her a small measure of peace."

The mention of the mysterious turning process made Lara's toes curl. The wind whipped her hair around her face, turning her breath to white mist.

"Thank you," Tristan said, sounding as if he genuinely meant it.

Annabelle waved her hand in the air. "Don't mention it." She set out for the edge of the meadow, carefully avoiding the dead vampires and any obvious puddles of blood.

Lara watched her until she was out of sight. "What about them?" she asked, pointing to the corpses. Every piece of vampire fiction she'd ever read spoke of vampires turning to dust after being impaled with a wooden stake, yet these remained whole.

"The sun will take care of them," Alexander answered. "And since the old woman wasn't concerned about neighbors stumbling in before then, I'm not either."

Tristan wrapped his arm around Lara's waist and pushed her gently toward the open door of the house. "Let's go in. You're freezing."

She nodded wordlessly. Together they made their way inside. The door closed behind them, just as it had in Katherine's memory, with a finality that echoed through the small room.

Lara walked to the flames dancing in the hearth and spread her palms out to warm her hands. Footsteps fell behind her. A man's shadow loomed immense on the stone wall. Hands reached out for her coat and she shrugged out of it, trembling as her thin blouse stuck to her sweat-soaked skin.

"We need to get you out of those clothes," Tristan said, dipping his fingers to caress her ribs. She gasped when he cupped her full, straining breasts. Moisture flooded her cunt, dampening the crotch of her panties and making the cotton fabric stick to her folds.

"Here?" she gasped. "With your brothers?"

Tristan's chuckle sent a rush of heat pooling low in her belly. "We all need to be present when we turn you, and this isn't like before. Trust me when I tell you that at the moment of turning, you'll want to be as immersed in pure pleasure as you can possibly be." His fingers worked at the small buttons of her shirt. He pulled the blouse off and bent his head to place a soft kiss at the curve of her neck. "That's where we come in."

"All of you," she repeated, still not fully comprehending what was about to happen. Arousal dimmed her thoughts, chased the logical arguments from her mind.

Tristan unhooked her bra. The straps slid down her arms. His fingers moved to the button at the waistband of her jeans.

He slid his hands inside the elastic band of her panties and pushed everything off in one sweeping motion, gathering her boots and tearing them from her feet.

Nudity didn't normally bother Lara, but this wasn't like being on display at Bitter Sweet where men were allowed to look but not touch. Here she felt vulnerable, and judging by the constant ache thrumming in her pussy, more aroused than she'd ever been.

She turned in Tristan's arms, sucking in a sharp breath when she realized he was naked too. Over his shoulder, she glimpsed Hayden and Alexander standing on either side of the door, their clothes crumpled in a mess of fabric at their feet.

Blood no longer covered the hard, sleek flesh of their bodies. She glanced at the small basin that lay in a corner of the room, noting the rippling red-stained surface of the water. Having already witnessed Tristan's abilities, the speed with which they'd cleaned themselves no longer surprised her.

Lara's heart pounded wildly as her focus shifted from broad shoulders to the planes of their chests then lower to flat abs and finally—*finally*—settled on the pure masculine flesh between their legs.

Hayden's cock jutted proudly from a mass of dark brown curls. Long and thick, it rivaled Tristan's in shape and size. In contrast, Alexander's was longer and thinner but just as mouthwatering. Both men watched her with interest, their fangs peeking from between their full lips.

"Mmm… You like what you see, don't you?"

Lara felt her face heat at Tristan's words. She hadn't realized she'd been rubbing her cunt against his thigh until he'd spoken and now embarrassment slithered down her spine, settling in the pit of her stomach.

"I'm sorry. It's just that I didn't… I couldn't have expected—"

"Shhh." Tristan's hands slid down her back and cupped her ass. He pressed her body closer and pushed his leg higher to grind against her mound. "Tonight, you have to let go of your inhibitions. And you have to trust us." He nipped at her earlobe and a flood of sensations drifted down her skin. "We won't hurt you."

She whimpered as his fingers trailed a path up the inside of her thigh then dipped in the crease of her ass. Pulling back slightly, Lara gave him access to her overheated cunt. Tristan's fingers delved within her slit. Her cream coated his hand and he used her natural juices to lubricate a path to the tight hole of her anus.

He shoved a finger inside slowly, allowing her muscles to adjust to the intrusion. "Have you ever been fucked here before, Lara?" Tristan asked, his voice velvety and smooth as honey.

She shook her head. "No." The word came out on a sigh and her eyelids began to drift closed as his finger slid deeper inside. Then her eyes snapped open. Alexander moved from his spot against the wall. She watched him circle the wooden table in the middle of the room and come to stand behind her.

"Alex knows how to pleasure a woman's ass." Tristan took a step back. For a moment, the loss of his body against hers was disorienting and infinitely alarming.

Then Alexander splayed his hands against the base of her spine, the tips of his fingers nudging her cheeks open.

"You're wet enough for all of us, aren't you, baby?" Alexander whispered in her ear as he trailed his hand through her folds to gather some of her moisture.

Lara didn't answer. She didn't have to. Her cunt clenched and when her muscles relaxed, another wave of fresh cream dripped down her inner thigh.

Alexander didn't content himself with just one finger. He pushed two inside the tight rosebud of her ass, making her cry out.

Tristan's eyebrows furrowed over his green eyes. "Are you hurt?"

Lara licked her suddenly dry lips. Her knees buckled as Alexander began to push his fingers in and out of her anus, mimicking the act of fucking. Instinctively, she shoved her ass back and found her own rhythm, meeting him thrust for thrust. "No," she gasped.

Tristan grinned. "Good girl. Now come with me."

Lara stumbled as she followed Tristan, Alexander's fingers still working their magic on her inner muscles. He led them to a woven blanket he'd spread out on the floor. Two pillows stacked on top of each other lay in the middle.

"Lie down," Tristan commanded.

Lara's heart thrummed painfully against her rib cage. Alexander stepped away, releasing her from the agonizing pleasure he'd delivered to her inner channel. She did as she was told and lay on her back, the pillows propped beneath her hips.

"Lift your legs," Alexander said. "I want your heels close to that hot ass of yours."

Lara didn't question the command, though somewhere in the back of her mind she wondered when she'd become so eager to please these men she'd only just met.

A few days ago she'd have thought giving any man so much control was beyond her. Worse yet, she figured women who allowed themselves to submit were beyond contempt. She'd believed she'd never be like them. Now lying here, her inner walls clenched in anticipation as she spread her thighs wide open, she knew better.

Hayden moved from his spot at the door.

"My brother's going to lick your pussy," Tristan said. "He's going to make you come and you're going to let him."

Hayden kneeled between her legs, his mouth just inches away from her hungry, needy cunt.

"Please," she breathed, thrusting her hips forward.

Her swollen labia fluttered as his tongue swept out and lapped at her slit. She shut her eyes tightly closed and screamed, her voice echoing off the stone walls. The rush of release hit with an unexpected intensity, tearing through her body, burrowing deep in her cunt and blasting a stream of warm, delicious heat through every nerve ending.

Something nudged her lips. She opened her eyes and her mouth in unison, accepting the cock thrust forward. She looked up — way up — into Alexander's eyes.

"That it, baby. Suck Alex's cock," Tristan encouraged.

Lara's eyelids drifted closed against the myriad sensations assaulting her from all sides. She didn't know how much more of this she could take. Hayden's wet mouth clamped around her pussy — his tongue, teeth and lips all working together to summon another orgasm from her already drained core.

She circled the velvety-smooth tip of Alexander's cock with her tongue then drew it fully inside her mouth, his musky taste flooding her senses with another jolt of arousal.

A third tongue swirled around her bellybutton then dipped inside, making her tremble.

Tristan.

"I'm here, baby."

She knew he'd heard her and the reassuring richness of his voice allowed her to suck harder on Alexander's cock. The thick shaft expanded even farther inside her mouth, filling her, drowning her in the salty flavor of pre-cum dripping from the slit.

Tristan squeezed one of her tender nipples between thumb and forefinger. Pleasure-pain drifted through her breast, making her arch her back.

Hayden nipped her inner thigh, just as he had in her dream. This time there was no fear, no terrorizing agony. He blew a cold stream of air over her moistened pussy then circled the swollen nub of her clit with the tip of his tongue.

Tristan tugged at her nipple. Alex pulled his cock out of her lips then slowly edged it back inside. He pushed in and out of her mouth with slow, practiced thrusts.

It was too much. Much too much. A second orgasm slammed into her. Lara whimpered as her body shook from the onslaught of sensation.

And then for a moment, it was over. Alexander drew his cock from her lips. Hayden pushed back on his heels. Tristan…

She opened her eyes, wildly scanning the area around her. "Tristan?"

He circled her wrist with his fingers and tugged her to her feet. "Right here, baby. Just as I said. I'd never leave you."

She almost sobbed at the certainty in his words. Then she gazed into his eyes and saw the concern glistening in his normally confident gaze. "Are you absolutely sure you want to do this?"

Lara's heart clenched. "Yes. More than anything. Yes."

She saw the broad set of his shoulders relax. "Okay then." He placed a kiss to her forehead, the infinitely tender act at odds with the lust-filled scenario they'd been acting out.

"Sit," he said.

Lara glanced down at the blanket. Alexander was splayed out of his back, one hand holding his cock, the other cupping his balls. He grinned up at her. "I'm ready when you are."

She swallowed hard. Her inner muscles tightened and she knew instantly he didn't want her pussy wrapped around his cock.

He wanted her ass.

And, God help her, she was going to give it to him.

Tristan held her elbow, helping her keep her balance as she squatted over Alexander's cock.

"Relax, sweetheart," Tristan whispered. "Alex will go slow. I promise."

She nodded, knowing she was in good hands. "I trust you. All of you."

Alex dipped his fingers within her slit, gathering some of her natural moisture. She glanced between her legs and watched him slick his shaft with the creamy lubrication. His erection glistened, the mushroom head flushed and eager to enter her.

Tristan kneeled in front of her, holding her gaze. She lost herself in the depths of his bottomless eyes, clinging to the reassurance he offered.

"That's it, baby," he murmured. "Let Alex have you. Let him open you and stretch you slowly with his cock."

While he spoke, Tristan reached between her legs and spread her labia apart. Delving inside, he explored her slippery depths, sending a shudder through her taut body.

The tip of Alex's cock nudged her ass open and she gasped, holding her breath against the pain she knew was inevitable. Tristan's thumb danced over her clit. Erotic sensations flooded her body, tightening her nipples, making her inner walls flutter in anticipation.

The first few inches of Alex's shaft slid inside her body and she felt her muscles stretch to accommodate him. The pain she'd expected flashed through her but it rode in on unexpected streams of pleasure.

Her breath hitched in her throat. She gritted her teeth and lowered herself on Alex's cock, her eyes never leaving Tristan's.

"That's it, baby. Let it happen."

"You feel so good," Alex whispered. He clamped his palms against her hips to steady her as he buried his thick girth inside her ass inch by inch.

"Oh wow," Lara murmured at last when his hips slammed against her ass cheeks and she knew she'd taken all of him. "That's amazing."

Tristan grinned, showing off his fangs. "That's the idea."

He dropped to his knees between their spread legs. His cock speared the air, hard as granite. Lara reached out and cupped his balls in her palm. "Will you fuck me?" The raw need in her voice surprised her. She cleared her throat and tried again but the words still held a whimper that sounded embarrassingly like a plea. "Will you fuck my pussy?"

Tristan parted her folds with the hard ridge of his cock. "What do you think?"

"Yes," she murmured, leaning back against Alexander's firm chest. "Yes."

Hayden kneeled at her side. His cock was close enough to her lips that she could swipe her tongue over it but he didn't pressure her to do so. Lara brought her hands up and enveloped his shaft in both palms then led him toward her mouth.

Tristan entered her, the sensation of two cocks filling her ass and pussy making her gasp in pure, unadulterated pleasure. She sucked Hayden's shaft, lost in a world of euphoric sensation.

Tristan's hips rocked against hers. Beneath her, Alexander matched their rhythm, as did Hayden, and soon they were rocking her from every side, filling her, *completing* her.

She shut her eyes tightly and rode the wave of ecstasy until it crested. When it came, her orgasm slammed hard into every muscle, tightening her limbs, clenching her hands tightly around Hayden's ass.

Hayden came next, his seed spilling into her mouth and dripping down her throat. Tristan and Alexander followed in quick succession. Through her own dizzying orgasm, she felt them, heard them cry out in the midst of their release.

And then the terror hit.

She'd felt it enough to recognize it for what it was the moment it slammed into her gut and clenched her inner muscles. Tears leaked beneath her closed eyelids.

She wanted to speak, to warn Tristan that it was happening again, but she didn't get the chance. He reached up to pinch her right nipple between thumb and forefinger.

The added sensation triggered a second orgasm, which rocked her body, jolting her just after the first wave of climax streamed through her. Intense vibrations of pure bliss flooded her nerve endings and mingled with the fear suffusing her mind.

Fangs sunk into her neck, her inner thigh, the inside of her elbow. The sharp stabs of pain traveled through her body, lancing through her like burning swords. They weakened her, made her tremble. Hayden's cock popped out of her mouth, his cum still leaking down her chin.

She opened her eyes through a groggy fog. Tangling one hand in Tristan's hair, she fought to push him off her, to get his fangs out of her flesh, but to no avail. She felt her blood rushing out of her veins. The pain increased, jolting her, ripping a scream from her throat.

She clawed at Tristan's back, kicked and flailed, eager to connect with anyone's body, needing to be free of the incessant agony surging through her body.

Darkness edged in. It enveloped her, sweeping over her naked form with soft, shadowy tendrils. Her head lolled back on her shoulders.

This is what death feels like.

It consumed her from within then blanketed her in a shroud she knew she could never escape.

And then fingers pried her jaw open. She struggled against them, strove to keep her lips firmly pressed together. But they were too strong. The massive blood loss had drained all the fight from her body.

She gave in.

Thick, metallic liquid filled her mouth. She gagged on it then writhed as it slid down her throat. She gulped, swallowing it down. A rush of heat warmed her veins.

Clamping her mouth around the flesh being offered to her, she sucked deeply, drowning in the coppery flavor of blood.

When he pulled his wrist away, she groped for it, but it was quickly replaced with another gushing vein. She drank eagerly, tasting the slightly sweeter flavor of Hayden's blood. And then that was gone too and a third, slightly tangy coppery taste rushed down her throat.

Suddenly she was no longer alone. Alexander, Hayden and Tristan were there, holding her, supporting her.

She could hear their thoughts—feel their emotions. She knew their deepest, darkest desires. An onslaught of sensations pounded through her with every gulp of blood. Curling her fingers around Alexander's wrist, she drank from him, sinking slowly in a sea of primal, dark need.

At once, Lara knew how Hayden had felt each time he'd watched his mate perish. She felt his sorrow, his anguish, his fear, that he'd forsaken every opportunity given to him.

She heard Alexander's thoughts, his envy warring with genuine happiness for his brother. Unlike Hayden, he'd never met his mate. He believed a woman meant for him didn't exist. Until that night, he'd taken comfort in knowing that Tristan hadn't found his chosen one either, but no longer. Now he was alone, the only Chance brother to be denied even a stab at a life by his mate's side.

Then as Tristan's memories poured into her, she saw herself through his eyes. She felt his lust, his animalistic need for her. She tasted his desire. She heard the desperation in his voice when she'd collapsed at his feet upon entering Annabelle's cavern. She knew without a doubt that he loved her as much she loved him.

She understood his concern, his fear that she'd falter in the face of such a dramatic change and he'd lose her as he'd lost his first wife. His memories flooded her with knowledge. The feeding requirements registered in her mind and she knew she'd be able to handle everything that being a vampire entailed, even sharing meals and delivering sexual bliss to those who shared their blood. It was a fair trade, she thought. An earth-shattering orgasm in return for life-giving sustenance.

She yearned to reassure Tristan she wasn't as fragile as his wife had been. As she blinked her eyes open and pushed Alexander's wrist away from her mouth, another certainly slammed into her, sending her thoughts reeling.

Her father had been behind the assassination attempts.

Chapter Fifteen

** හ**

Lara wasn't sure what she'd expected to find upon returning to New York, but the complete and utter sameness of things wasn't it. An hour before the stores closed on Christmas Eve, the sidewalks bustled with activity. People ran everywhere in a constant state of frenzy as they hurried to finish their last-minute shopping.

A thin layer of snow blanketed the sidewalk and turned the streets into slush-covered skating rinks. The wind blew cold, seeping under clothes and running its chill fingertips over every inch of uncovered flesh.

Lara no longer felt it.

Clouds covered the moon, blotted out the stars. By all accounts, New York should have been swathed in darkness but the neon glow of holiday lights made the city glow brighter than it would in the middle of the afternoon on a warm July day. In the distance the Empire State Building sparkled against the black night sky.

Lara sighed and crossed the street, shoving her hands into the pockets of her new leather coat. It didn't seem right that nothing about the city had changed when everything about *her* had been permanently, unequivocally altered.

She pushed through the revolving doors leading into the Montgomery Suites Corporate Headquarters. "'Evening, Mike. Are they up there?"

The security guard paled. She could smell his fear, an acrid, bitter scent that left a bad taste in her mouth.

"Yes, but they warned me not to let you —"

"Thanks. That's all I needed to know."

214

The elevator doors slid open as she pushed the button. As they closed, she saw Mike reach for the phone at his post. It didn't matter. Let him warn her father and brother. There wasn't a place they could go she wouldn't find them.

Lara tapped her foot impatiently as the elevator climbed toward the thirtieth floor. An old Michael Jackson tune rang out in sharp, electronic beats, flooding the lift. She glanced to her right and for a moment, she was startled to catch a glimpse of her reflection. Then she smiled, revealing sharp fangs protruding from her blood-red lips.

Although Tristan had tried to give her a course in vampirism as soon as she awoke to her new life, Lara had only wanted the basic lessons. She'd already gleaned a lot of vital information during the act of turning. Since then, she'd learned that once mated, vampires shared everything.

That evening, Tristan had taken her with him to feed. As they'd searched the streets for a suitable choice, he'd explained that from now on, they'd feed together from the same human. A vampire who took a human without his mate present was in effect committing adultery. Since the act of sharing a victim's blood with a mate was intensely intimate and blissfully satisfying, she understood the need to remain faithful and always share the experience.

Lara smiled, her heartbeat quickening at the memory of sinking her fangs into a woman's throat earlier that night. She'd thrust her fingers inside the woman's wet pussy while Tristan sucked on a taut nipple. She could still taste the sweet metallic flavor of her blood lingering on her tongue.

For now until the end of time, she and Tristan were one. Their hunger, their needs, even their sexual bliss would be forever dependent on the other.

She wouldn't have it any other way.

The loud ding of the elevator bell announced her arrival. As the doors began to open, she saw Elias careen away from the elevator and launch himself at the fire exit. The door didn't budge beneath his weight.

"That's for emergencies only," Lara whispered in his ear.

He jumped and started to turn but she clamped her hand around his neck and pushed his face into the door.

"L-Lara. I didn't see you."

She grinned. "Of course you didn't."

Tristan hadn't even had to teach her how to move faster than thought. The innate ability came as naturally to her as breathing or the need for blood.

"What are you doing here?" he squeaked, his words muffled against the metal Exit sign.

"Actually, I'm looking for our father. You wouldn't happen to know where he is, would you?"

"The boardroom." He gasped as she tightened her grip. "Honest. He's in the boardroom."

Lara sighed. "He would be, wouldn't he? He's probably preparing to receive me like the head of state receives a supplicant. He'd never lower himself to run from me."

She didn't wait for Elias to answer. Instead, she pulled back and slammed his forehead against the door. Elias crumpled to the ground. She watched him fall dispassionately, surprised at how little satisfaction she derived from that. She'd been wanting to do it for years.

Flexing the fingers of her right hand, she walked toward the boardroom. She didn't run or use her superhuman abilities to catch her father off guard. It wouldn't matter, anyway. The CEO of Montgomery Suites, the man who learned the truth behind a vampire's existence and sent another squad of vampires to do his dirty work wouldn't flinch from his own daughter.

"Are you here to call in Chance's favor?" Stephen asked when Lara leaned against the doorframe.

"Word travels fast."

"About my whore of a daughter and her unnatural lover? It was all over the news. Or don't you read the papers?"

He slid a newspaper across the table. From where she stood, Lara could make out the headline. "Saint To Marry Heiress" it read, and below it, in smaller font, "Hands off, ladies. One of New York's hottest bachelors was just taken off the market by the daughter of hotel mogul Stephen Montgomery."

Lara released a breath she hadn't known she'd been holding. Judging by her father's expression, she'd expected the paper to have revealed the truth about Tristan's nature—and hers. Though knowing Stephen, this bit of news was just as unpleasant to him...probably more so.

"I tried to protect you. I sent you away from him." Stephen slammed a fist against the table. Lara didn't flinch.

"Right, sending assassins to murder Tristan was all for my own good."

"You don't know what you're doing. I could never trust you to make your own decisions. The *right* decisions."

Lara fisted her hands. Her nails dug into her palms. "Killing the only man who has ever loved me would have been in my own best interest. Is that what you're trying to say?"

Stephen snorted. "Love? Listen to you. You speak like a child. Love's an illusion. It was created to keep wives in their proper place while husbands fucked everything on two legs. It's an emotion meant to control."

That's it. I'm coming in there.

Lara narrowed her eyes, the only outward indication of the bond she shared with her mate.

I can handle it.

The pause stretched on for a beat then another. *I know you can. I worry, that's all.*

This time, Lara allowed herself a smile. She hated being "protected" by men who sought to control her but it was different with Tristan. He didn't want to rule her life or to steer the course of her every decision. He genuinely wanted to keep her safe and by his side—forever.

She couldn't fault him for that. In fact, she loved him for it.

But it didn't mean she was going to let him get away with it. She had to set some ground rules in this relationship and she would, just as soon as she wrapped up the last of the unfinished business pertaining to her old life.

Without warning, she dashed to her father's side as fast as thought and leaned over him, her hand flattening his arm against the chair's armrest. A small gasp was the only sound Stephen allowed himself to make. He clamped his lips together and glared at her, fury roiling in his black eyes.

"You would know all about control, wouldn't you?" Lara said. "But you're wrong. Despite growing up with you, I know what love is. I feel it every time Tristan comes near me. I felt it that night, right here in this boardroom." She made the effort to lean closer, though the unmistakable tang of the fear her father fought to hide assaulted her nostrils. "You knew that though, didn't you? That's why you ordered him killed."

"You have all the answers." Stephen sneered. "You tell me."

"Listen to me and listen good, because I'm only going to say this once. If you ever so much as *think* about hurting me, Tristan or any of his brothers, I'll make sure you don't live to see another sunrise. Are we clear?"

Stephen's nostrils flared. Lara could practically feel the raw fury that surged just beneath the surface. But underneath that was something else—a gut-clenching terror roiling deep in his gut. It quickened his heartbeat and sent the blood pouring through his veins in a frenzied *whoosh*. The sound made her fangs extend farther. She pressed them against the pulsing vein in his neck. It took all her self-control not to break the skin. "Are. We. Clear."

"Fine. I'll rip up my contract and return the money. This makes us even."

Lara tossed her head back and laughed, the sound echoing throughout the room. Stephen started at her sudden mirth.

"What makes you think we're anywhere close to even? You're not tearing up anything until Tristan tells you to. I had to argue with him for an hour to come see you alone. Next time, he won't be nearly as generous. And frankly, I wouldn't deny him the satisfaction of watching you squirm."

Stephen's muscles stiffened. He hunched his shoulders in frustrated anger but the pure hatred seething in his eyes was like nothing she'd ever seen before, and she'd grown up learning to anticipate every angry glance he threw her way. "Go then. Be a good little undead whore."

Lara shook her head. A few minutes ago, that comment would have enraged her. It would probably have even made her test her newfound strength on her father's weak, mortal body.

But now, knowing he was as scared of her as he'd ever been of anyone was enough to stifle the violent urge. She finally had everything she'd ever wanted from her father—a grudging respect for her abilities.

She'd always assumed she'd get it by working hard and proving herself to him. Instead, it had been as easy as giving in to her destiny.

And to Tristan.

* * * * *

"How'd it go?" Tristan leaned against the door of his limo. A muscle pulsed in his jaw from grinding his teeth the entire time Lara had been inside the building.

She stopped two steps away, close enough for her body to tantalize him with its lush curves, yet far enough away to make a point. "You shouldn't have followed me."

"I didn't follow you…exactly."

She rolled her eyes. "Either you trust me to take care of myself or you don't. Which is it?"

Tristan flashed his best lopsided grin in an attempt try to disarm her. Judging by the way she crossed her arms over her breasts, it didn't work.

"Fine. I followed you. But not because I thought you couldn't handle Stephen Montgomery."

"Why then?"

"Did it occur to you that he may have hired more assassins than just those he sent to Midwich? What if he had the rest of them waiting inside that building for me?" He reached out and trailed his knuckles across her cheek. "Or for you."

Her eyelids drifted closed. She groaned and rubbed the bridge of her nose. "I didn't even consider that possibility. I just thought… I mean, I *had* to do this." When she opened her eyes, they glistened with unshed tears. "You must think I'm an idiot."

Tristan put his arm around her slender shoulders and drew her close. "I think you're incredibly brave."

Her soft curves molded against the firm planes of his chest and heat stirred in his groin. Tristan activated the link between them and projected a mental image of himself and his brothers writhing against Lara's slick, sweat-soaked skin, riding her even as they rode the wings of death.

Your death.

She gazed up at him, her eyes lit from within by a radiant, intense glow. "I don't know if I'll ever really get used to hearing you in my head."

He ran his thumb over her full lower lip. She opened her mouth and drew it inside, nipping his skin with the tip of a sharp fang. Blood welled to the surface and she licked it away, sweeping her tongue over the wound to seal it closed.

Tristan groaned. "Then you better find a way to get used to it, baby. I'm not going anywhere."

She chuckled and slid her hand around his neck, bringing his mouth down to hers. The taste of his blood mingling with her own unique flavor nearly sent him to his knees.

He cupped her face in his hands and slid his tongue between her luscious, parted lips, feasting on her. Through the bond, he heard her moan, though the sound was lost inside his mouth.

I love you.

Something inside Tristan shattered as her thought slid through his mind. He broke the kiss. "Say it. Out loud. I need to hear you say it."

Lara ran a finger down his chest, her long eyelashes hiding the depths of her hazel eyes. He tilted her head, needing to see her — all of her.

"To hell with this." Patience had never been one of his virtues.

With a low growl, Tristan yanked open the door to the limo. He couldn't remember ever moving faster in his entire existence. Wrapping his arms around Lara's waist, he pulled her inside and slammed the door behind them.

He pushed her down on the bench facing the front of the car and kneeled before her, shoving the hem of her skirt around her waist with one hand. With the other, he pushed her thin cotton panties to the side and dipped his finger inside her slit.

"Say it," he repeated, two fingers nudging the entrance to her hot, moist cunt.

She grabbed the back of his head. She opened her mouth to speak then her eyes went wide and she pointed to something behind him. "Tristan, I don't think—"

He lifted her legs off the ground and placed them over his shoulders. His tongue replaced his hand, and he swept a path along her slick cunt. She trembled, her hips writhing off the bench to meet his mouth.

Her arousal flooded his senses, drowning him in the taste and feel of her. His tongue worked in small, sensual circles over her folds and she wriggled her irresistible ass, bringing his mouth closer to her clit with every stroke.

Say it.

"I—" Lara gasped as he slid two fingers inside her. With his free hand, he lowered his zipper, undoing his pants.

Yes?

"I really think you should—"

A growl rang out through the back of the limo and it took Tristan a moment to realize it was his own. He cupped her ass with both hands, rose from the floor and switched positions, taking her place and positioning her over his throbbing cock.

It all happened so fast, Lara barely had time to breathe. He saw the shock glistening in her eyes as he impaled her on his shaft, unable to hold back a moment longer. She bunched the fabric of his suit jacket in her fingers and cried out as he thrust into her, again and again, loving the way her tight inner muscles clenched around his dick.

He brought his hand between them and lightly toyed with her clit.

"I love you, damn you," she whispered. Her moist heat squeezed his cock. "But—"

No buts.

He flicked the hard nub with his fingertip. Lara cried out, her pussy spasming and constricting around him, torturing his cock with every shuddering pulse. Her release triggered his own. He cried out as his seed jetted inside her. He held her close to his chest, feeling every tremble of her climax rip through her body.

Hayden used to say that the turning created a permanent bond between souls. Since that hadn't been his experience the one time he'd previously attempted to share himself with another, he'd never believed his brother's words.

Now as Lara clung to him, her curls sticking to the side of her sweat-drenched face, he understood. He could feel her — all of her. He knew the emotions roiling inside her as though they were his own. He didn't even have to activate the bond to hear her thoughts.

"Oh yeah, hotshot?" Her breath warmed his ear. She nipped his earlobe lightly. "Then why do I get the feeling you had no idea we had an audience?"

Lara's words slammed into him, jolting him back to reality. He grimaced as he peered around her. The privacy window separating the back of the limo from the cab was still lowered. He vaguely remembered leaving it that way when he gave Tom instructions to follow Lara.

Good old Tom, who'd been with him for twenty years and often bragged that nothing his employer did surprised him anymore, now gaped in opened-mouthed wonder.

From the seat beside him, Marie reached out and snapped his jaw closed. "Didn't anyone ever tell you it's not polite to stare?"

Tristan growled, tightening his grip on Lara. He was grateful for her skirt and the fact that his cock remained sheathed inside her tight pussy. With one hand, he reached out and pushed the button to raise the divider.

Marie wiggled her fingertips, waving as the barrier separated them.

Lara chuckled against Tristan's neck. "I'm guessing she's the one I have to thank for the lovely wedding announcement in today's paper."

Tristan gritted his teeth. "Thank her fast. She may not live that long."

Lara brushed a strand of hair out of his eyes and tucked it behind his ear. The smile was gone. She peered down at him, her dark eyes blazing with intensity. "Living with you is never going to be dull, is it?"

"Never," he promised her. "Besides, you won't just be living with me. You'll be working with me too. I can think of at least a few men in New York who'd give their right eye to be rescued from financial hardship by you."

She wrinkled her nose. "I'm not a big fan of eyeballs. Too squishy."

Tristan laughed. "Then we'll find you a different body part to play with. And if you grow bored of coming in to work with me, there are plenty of distractions in New York. About half the city owes me a favor or two."

She grinned. "I see a lot of shopping in my future."

"Easy now." He slid a hand into the inside pocket of his jacket and pulled out a white, slightly crumpled envelope. "I can cash in on your IOU at any time too."

Lara grabbed the envelope and tore it once, down the middle. He didn't try to stop her but blew out a deep breath, feigning disappointment. "You still owe me."

She lowered her head and nipped the tender flesh of his throat. Her pussy tightened around his cock, the shaft raging to life at the sudden reminder of the hot, moist channel that held it in its grip.

"And I intend to pay my debt in full," she whispered, unbuttoning his shirt. "Every day of my life."

With or without an audience, she added silently.

Tristan grinned and leaned his head back against the bench, relaxing into his mate's caress. He couldn't remember ever being this happy. This…complete.

From somewhere far away, Hayden's voice grazed his thoughts.

I told you so.

Why an electronic book?

We live in the Information Age—an exciting time in the history of human civilization, in which technology rules supreme and continues to progress in leaps and bounds every minute of every day. For a multitude of reasons, more and more avid literary fans are opting to purchase e-books instead of paper books. The question from those not yet initiated into the world of electronic reading is simply: *Why?*

1. *Price.* An electronic title at Ellora's Cave Publishing and Cerridwen Press runs anywhere from 40% to 75% less than the cover price of the exact same title in paperback format. Why? Basic mathematics and cost. It is less expensive to publish an e-book (no paper and printing, no warehousing and shipping) than it is to publish a paperback, so the savings are passed along to the consumer.

2. *Space.* Running out of room in your house for your books? That is one worry you will never have with electronic books. For a low one-time cost, you can purchase a handheld device specifically designed for e-reading. Many e-readers have large, convenient screens for viewing. Better yet, hundreds of titles can be stored within your new library—on a single microchip. There are a variety of e-readers from different manufacturers. You can also read e-books on your PC or laptop computer. (Please note that Ellora's Cave does not endorse any specific brands.

You can check our websites at www.ellorascave.com or www.cerridwenpress.com for information we make available to new consumers.)

3. *Mobility.* Because your new e-library consists of only a microchip within a small, easily transportable e-reader, your entire cache of books can be taken with you wherever you go.

4. *Personal Viewing Preferences.* Are the words you are currently reading too small? Too large? Too... ANNOYING? Paperback books cannot be modified according to personal preferences, but e-books can.

5. *Instant Gratification.* Is it the middle of the night and all the bookstores near you are closed? Are you tired of waiting days, sometimes weeks, for bookstores to ship the novels you bought? Ellora's Cave Publishing sells instantaneous downloads twenty-four hours a day, seven days a week, every day of the year. Our webstore is never closed. Our e-book delivery system is 100% automated, meaning your order is filled as soon as you pay for it.

Those are a few of the top reasons why electronic books are replacing paperbacks for many avid readers.

As always, Ellora's Cave and Cerridwen Press welcome your questions and comments. We invite you to email us at Comments@ellorascave.com or write to us directly at Ellora's Cave Publishing Inc., 1056 Home Avenue, Akron, OH 44310-3502.

COMING TO A BOOKSTORE NEAR YOU!

ELLORA'S CAVE

Bestselling Authors Tour

UPDATES AVAILABLE AT

WWW.ELLORASCAVE.COM

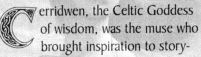

Discover for yourself why readers can't get enough of the multiple award-winning publisher Ellora's Cave.

Whether you prefer e-books or paperbacks, be sure to visit EC on the web at www.ellorascave.com

for an erotic reading experience that will leave you breathless.